PER AND JOURNEY

by

SUE BRIDGWATER

and

ALISTAIR MCGECHIE

First published in hardcover 1989 by Julia MacRae Books
Reset by DreamWorlds Publishing (New Edition) 2014

ISBN 978-0-9927472-2-0

Original Maps © Alistair McGechie
Cover design & artwork © Jan Hawke

Published by Eluth Publishing
in association with DreamWorlds Publishing

Printed by Ingram Spark

For
Andrew, Caitlin, Duncan and Martin

Contents

Preface

Skorn is an imaginary planet where various stories unfold, and Perian's Journey is the first of these. It has been the first step in bringing to life a world of lore and legend, myth and magic set in an imagined world of mountains, desert, sea and plain, which is Skorn.

We have many people to thank for our own story to date. It was the late Julia McCrae who published the first edition of Perian's Journey for Walker Books, and we remain grateful to her for her faith in us. Our families and friends have supported us throughout our years of work on the Skorn corpus, and have helped with reading and comments upon work in progress.

Our special thanks go to Jan Hawke of DreamWorlds Publishing, our mentor and supporter in the establishing of Eluth Publishing, and first among those who insisted it was time to bring more of Skorn to readers. This new edition of Perian's Journey was produced by Eluth Publishing, a new publishing house dedicated to making available the tales of Skorn.

Sue Bridgwater and Alistair McGechie, 2014

The East Sea

Prologue

Once, long ago, in the days when Skalwood spread down to the bank of the River Siannen, a traveller came from the deserts of the south. His name was Verumis and he was a wanderer, an outcast from his own land. He came to the green valley and lay down beside the gentle water and fell asleep upon the bank, in the hot afternoon. There he had a dream. He saw a flower growing beside a stream and he heard a voice saying:

"Know this for a sign. For all flowers fade and die in the heat. This flower burns, but it will never die."

And, as the voice fell silent, the flower burst into flames and gave out a brilliant light but was not consumed by the fire. When Verumis woke up he remembered his dream, and looked about him at the lovely valley of the Siannen, and he said:

"I will stay here and dwell by the river, in this green valley. For the meaning of my dream is that this is a good place, where flowers are not withered by the fiery sun."

And so he built a house by the river Siannen and he prospered. As the years passed more people came to live close by and a town grew up about his house. He made a banner to fly above the town and the banner showed a burning flower. The town became known as The Home of Verumis or, in the language of those times, La Verumis. Through the long ages the name of the town has changed and now it is known as Lavrum; but the banner of the Flaming Flower, crafted by Verumis, still waves in the gentle wind above its walls.

BOOK 1

The Two Seeds

1 The Wizard

Long after the name of Verumis had passed into legend there were two brothers called Agravin and Montague. They lived together in a small log house at the foot of a great mountain, near the northern edge of Skalwood. Agravin was large and serious, and Montague was slightly built and laughed a lot. They had one sister who had married and lived in a nearby town. The land the brothers lived on was poor and they had to work hard all day every day to grow enough food to eat. They had one field each and the farm was known as Two Fields Farm.

Each day they would walk, side by side, from their house along the edge of the forest to their fields to work. They would work alone all morning. Agravin laboured steadily keeping his eyes upon his work, while Montague would often look up at the mountains or peer into the forest hoping to see some rare bird or wild creature looking back at him. After eating their simple lunch they would work separately all afternoon and then return home together.

One day, while walking past the trees on the way home they heard a voice cry out:

"Help me, please!"

They looked round, but nobody was there.

'Perhaps it is a ghost, or a bad spirit," said Agravin, looking nervously about.

"Perhaps it is," said Montague with a laugh. "Let's go and see."

They left the path slowly and moved towards the voice

"Help me, please," it said again. They were getting nearer. There was a large tree in a small clearing and the voice seemed to come from behind it. They walked round the tree but there was no-one there.

"Help me, please."

"Where are you?" said Montague crossly.

"I am in the tree, trapped by magic. Will you set me free?"

"Yes, but how can we do that?" asked Agravin.

"You must join hands to make a ring around the tree trunk," said the voice. "Have you done that?"

"Yes," said the brothers.

"Good. Now you must unsay the binding word. Say 'Aramek!' together loudly."

Agravin and Montague felt very foolish holding hands around the tree. Neither could see the other so Montague counted so that they could say the magic word in unison.

"Aramek!" they both shouted.

At first nothing happened, then the branches of the tree began to shake and there was a sound like falling leaves. The brothers could see nothing because their noses were still pressed up against the bark of the tree.

"Thank you," said the voice, from behind Agravin. "Now it is safe to break the circle."

They unclasped their hands and turned towards the voice. Standing there was a beautiful young man in fine clothes, smiling and holding out his arms. The brothers were awed by this vision of richness and authority, and they moved forward, each taking a hand, and knelt before the lordly youth.

He thanked them again and told them that he was a wizard and had been bound into the tree by an evil sorceress.

"I am a servant of the Lady Siannor in her eternal battle against evil. I must return to her now. But before I go I would like to reward you for your kindness."

Agravin and Montague were amazed at all this, for it was years since they had seen anybody near their remote farm and they knew nothing of magic. They listened open-mouthed, still on their knees. The young wizard reached into a secret pocket in his robe and took something out. He held his hand out and showed the brothers two tiny black dots.

"These are seeds. There is one for each of you. I hope that they will bring you happiness when they have grown. But what they grow into will depend on where you plant them. If you plant them here they will give some benefit and some disappointment. The higher up they are planted the greater the joy and the greater the sorrow. If they grow in the highest possible place they will give ecstasy and great pain. It is up to you where you plant them. I must bid you farewell now. Good fortune be with you for your kindness."

The brothers took their seeds, then the young wizard stepped back, turned round and faded away before their eyes. The wood suddenly seemed dark and Agravin and Montague hurried home, each clutching his seed in his hand.

The next morning they woke up as the sun rose, and on the table they found the two seeds.

"Did that really happen yesterday?" said Agravin when he saw them. "I thought it must be a dream."

"Yes. I can hardly believe it. We must decide what to do with the seeds," said Montague.

"It is a good time for planting," replied Agravin. "I will plant mine in my field this morning."

"He said that it would be better higher up. I think I'll go up to the mountain slopes to plant mine."

Agravin looked anxious. "He also said it would be worse higher up. Why don't you plant yours here too?"

"No. I want to see what happens higher up. My crops will be all right for a few days while I'm away. I'll go today."

He packed some food into a bag and put his seed into a little pouch on his belt and set out towards the mountain, waving to Agravin as he went out of sight. Agravin looked slightly worried as he closed the door of their house and went to his field to work and to plant his magic seed.

As Montague walked towards the great mountain he sang, for it was a beautiful spring day. By evening he was already climbing and if he turned round he could see the valley, where he lived, stretching out below him. On the second day the path was steep and by the third day he could no longer walk but had to scramble on all fours. As the sun went down, Montague looked around for somewhere to plant his seed. But the ground was hard and dry, and nothing would grow there.

"I'll have to go further up," he said to himself. He climbed for three more days and as he went the way became steeper and harder. He stopped and looked round, but there was nowhere to plant the seed.

"I'll have to go further up," he said again, and carried on climbing. After three more days he came near to the top of the mountain. He stopped and looked around. This time he saw some green grass, went towards it and found a little spring watering some rich dark soil.

"This must be the place. I'll plant the seed here," he said and he planted his seed there and then. This must be the highest soil in the world, he thought.

The next day he started back down the mountain. The homeward journey was easy and pleasant and Montague sang as he went. Sometimes he would sit quietly by a stream for a while to watch the dippers diving or the shy deer drinking. Nine days later he arrived back at the little house just as Agravin was returning from his day's work.

"Oh, it's good to see you again," Agravin said as they were eating their supper. "When you did not come home after a week I thought you must be dead. Foreign places are dangerous and we are not used to danger."

"It was not dangerous," replied his brother. "But I could not find the right place to plant the seed until I was nearly at the top of the mountain. There I found good soil where the seed should grow well."

"But harvesting will be difficult," said Agravin seriously. Montague just laughed.

"But how is your seed, my dear brother?" he asked.

"It's coming along nicely. You'll see it tomorrow."

The next day they got up as usual and went to the fields. First they both went to Agravin's field to look at his magic plant. Montague was amazed to see a tree as tall as him.

"Has it grown so tall already?" he asked.

As the days went by Agravin's tree grew larger and larger until it shaded most of the field. And before long blossom appeared and then a fine crop of fruit. The brothers worked together climbing the tree and collecting the harvest in baskets.

When they had finished Agravin took a fruit and tasted it.

"Like a peach or an apple, but not like them."

Montague took a bite from one.

"This one tastes like dumplings and gravy."

They tried several more and found that they all had different flavours.

"There's no need to grow any other crops," said Agravin.

"It makes me wonder," said Montague, "what has become of my seed. I will take some of the fruit and go back up the mountain to see. Will you come with me?"

"No, I must stay and look after my tree," said Agravin.

So the next morning Montague filled a bag with fruit and set off alone to find the spring near the top of the mountain.

On the evening of the ninth day, after a hard climb, he came to the spring and the green haven on the rocky mountain-side. When he saw what had grown from his seed he was disappointed, for he had expected a tree like his brother's, perhaps even larger or with richer fruit, if that were possible. But all that he could see was a tangle of thorns and brambles, which had spread over the ground and grown no higher than his shoulder.

Evening was drawing in and in the gloom the dark mass of vegetation seemed horrible and ugly. But as the daylight faded Montague thought he saw a glow coming from within the thicket. He went closer, pulled some of the outer branches aside and peered into the depths of the dark tangle. He could just see a single shining flower. It was the colour of a flame; yellow and orange and blue, and it flickered faintly so that it seemed about to fade away. It was like porcelain and like silk. It seemed eternal and transitory, tantalising and reassuring.

Montague crouched, staring into the darkness, watching the beautiful flower.

When dawn came he realised that he had not moved all night and his body ached and his eyes were tired. He stretched and looked about him. The mountain and the sky looked wonderful to him and he felt a deep joy. He danced and sang happily, then scrambled to the top of the mountain and looked out over the whole world. He shouted his news:

"I have seen the flower! It is here on the mountain."

But nobody heard him.

He went back down to the bush to look at the flower again. Its light seemed dim against the daylight, but it was still the most exquisite vision. Montague was again transfixed so that time stood still.

"I must tell Agravin," he said to himself. "He must come and see it."

He took his bag and hurried down the mountain, occasionally dancing and leaping as he went and sometimes singing and shouting. Each rock, each tree, each little plant seemed beautiful to him as he passed it on his way. When he reached level ground after travelling day and night, he ran all the way home. He found Agravin sitting under his tree.

"You must come up the mountain and see the flower!" Montague shouted breathlessly as he came near the tree.

Agravin jumped up in surprise.

"What's wrong, brother? You look ill."

Montague told him about the wonderful flower, his words tumbling out breathlessly.

"Come, Agravin," he said. "You must come and see it. My poor words cannot tell you its beauty or the peace and joy it brings. It is the most wonderful thing in the world."

Agravin thought for a while with a serious expression on his face.

"No. I must look after my tree. Anyway, there are flowers here; in the wood, in the fields and round our home. Why should I climb the mountain just to see a flower?"

"This is not just any flower, Agravin. It is the perfect flower."

Agravin was nearly convinced and thought hard before deciding.

"No. I love my tree. And after all a flower is only a flower when all's said and done."

Montague was crestfallen. He sat with Agravin in the shade of the tree, eating the fruit and thinking. Suddenly he cheered up.

"I know!" he shouted. "If you will not come with me to see the flower, I will bring it to you!"

Agravin said that would be kind, as he would like to see it, but insisted that Montague rest for a few days as he looked worn out. Montague was impatient to be off but agreed to wait until the full moon before setting out.

"It will make the nights lighter. And besides, I must tell you all about my journey," he said.

The days were passed pleasantly by the brothers, trying the different fruits of the tree, talking and laughing together.

When the full moon came, Montague set off up the mountain with his bag of fruit. The mountain no longer seemed strange to him; he recognised landmarks on the way and the climb was not as difficult as it had been the first time.

As soon as he arrived at the bush he looked to check that the flower was still blooming. He had difficulty seeing it, as the brambles had grown thicker since his last visit, but the flower was still there, if anything more beautiful than he had remembered it. He immediately set to work trying to reach it. He had his knife with him and he tried to cut some of the thorny branches. They were very tough and it took him all day to get his head and shoulders into the thicket.

By the end of the next day he could just manage to crawl right into the bush but he could not quite reach the flower. By now his arms and face were badly torn by the thorns, but he did not notice the pain for as he got nearer to the flower he could see its beauty more clearly. Finally on the third day he was just able to reach the flower with his outstretched hands. He did not touch the delicate petals but, holding on to its stem with one hand, he cut it with his knife. The bush seemed to shudder and close in around him and he dropped the knife. But he held on to the stem and the flower remained undamaged. He started to back out of the bush holding the flower close to his chest so that it would not be harmed. As he moved, thorns ripped at his back, his arms and his face, but he shielded the flower and did not feel the pain. In this way he gradually extricated himself from the bush. Eventually he could feel his lower half escape and with a final pull he released himself. As he did so a thick briar covered with large thorns ripped across his face and he screamed with pain. Blood ran down the side of his face and he realised that his right eye had been ripped out. He ignored that and with his one good eye examined the flower carefully. It was undamaged, perfect. He wrapped it carefully in a damp cloth and placed it gently in his pouch. Then he went to the spring and bathed his torn body and bleeding face. He sat down, took out the flower and gazed at it again for a while.

Then he collapsed, exhausted, and slept for the rest of the day and all through the night.

The next day he tore strips from his shirt and bound up his wounded face and started down the mountain with the flower safely in his pouch. His body ached with every step, but as he neared home he felt better and his wounds were healing. Still Agravin was horrified when he saw him.

"Oh my brother, what have you done?" he exclaimed.

Montague smiled proudly.

"It's not as bad as it looks," he said, "and I have succeeded. Look."

He took the flower out of the pouch on his belt, laid it on the ground and unwrapped it for his brother to see. Agravin examined it with interest, but when Montague saw it, tears ran down his scarred face from his one eye. For while the flower was undamaged, its colours had faded and the edges of the petals were going brown. Montague howled with disappointed rage and fell to his knees. Agravin looked at him, uncomprehending.

"It is very lovely, Montague," he said. "Thank you for bringing it to me."

Montague looked up sadly at his brother.

"No, this is not the flower I saw up on the mountain. This is a dead body. All the light has gone out of it, and it has no power to comfort or inspire."

Agravin tried to console him.

"It's beautiful all the same. But I must say you should not have sacrificed so much to bring it here."

"You are right, Agravin: this was not worth the trouble. Oh, how I wish you had come with me to see this flower when it was alive."

Montague carefully wrapped the delicate bloom in its cloth and took it into the house.

Each year after that, one-eyed Montague would go up the mountain to see his bush, but no new flower ever grew within it. He would come down the mountain and roam about the countryside peering into tangled briar-patches and looking at flowers. He wandered about the mountain slopes and even ventured into Skalwood, where he saw many strange and beautiful things. He came to know the plants and animals of the region and when he returned home he told Agravin of his discoveries. Montague's field became overgrown but Agravin gladly gave his brother a share of the fruits of the tree. Montague always remembered the night he had spent gazing at the flame-like flower.

Agravin listened to his brother's stories and enjoyed them, but he would always say:

"Your field is getting out of hand, Montague. Tomorrow we must set to and start clearing the weeds." He himself never went far from his tree and grew fat on its fruit. The tree needed little tending and he spent most of summer sitting in its shade and most of winter sitting by the fire. One evening many years later when the two brothers were sitting in their warm little house, Agravin said:

"Do you ever think of that day when we rescued the young wizard?"

"Every day," answered Montague.

"I wonder what he would think about how we chose to plant our seeds. I think I have had more happiness from mine than you've had from yours. And yours cost you an eye. Though I sometimes wish I had not spent so much time looking after my tree and had seen more of the world."

"Yes. I believe I have seen more with my one eye than you have with two."

"Maybe, maybe. But if we needed only one eye we would not have been given two. In any case I have seen your flower and you have shared my fruit."

"Not really, brother. If you had travelled up the mountain with me you would have seen the flower's true beauty. And I have been glad enough to eat your fruit, but how much work did I do towards the care of the tree? We have not truly shared as brothers should."

There was a short silence while the two stared into the fire.

"Do you suppose," Agravin said slowly, "that one person could ever contrive to do both things? I mean, to enjoy the peace in the shade of the tree and yet dare the wild mountain slopes in search of beauty?"

"Why, Agravin," laughed his brother, "you are quite the philosopher. I wonder if anyone could?"

They sat quietly again for a while. Then Montague said,

"Brother, next spring we must invite Elyn to stay with us here at the farm. I have been concerned for her ever since we heard that she was widowed. It would be a fine thing for that lad of hers to grow up here, nourished by your good fruit. And we are getting on now, a helping hand would be welcome, and who better than our own niece?"

"It would be a big change for us. A young child about the place, won't that be noisy and troublesome?"

"Oh, Agravin. You met young Perian two years ago when we visited them in the town; a fat solemn baby, no trouble to anyone. It will do us good. I will tell him tales of the mountain, and you shall sit with him under the tree. Do say yes, brother."

"Oh, all right," said Agravin.

So Elyn and Perian came to live at Two Fields Farm. Elyn cared for her uncles and they delighted in Perian. Agravin would talk to him of sowing seed and storing crops, of how to build a log stack and how to mend a fence. Montague took him for walks and showed him hidden flowers and the tracks of wild animals, and told him of the high mountains and of dark Skalwood.

But before long Agravin died and his brother buried him under the tree. Montague died two years later and was laid beside his brother. Elyn was left to care for Perian alone.

2 Perian

It was during the following summer that the wizard's journeyings brought him to Skalwood again. He remembered the two young farmers who had rescued him so readily from the tree long ago. He had rewarded them with a magic seed apiece; to what use had they put their gifts? How were they? Surely their cottage lay somewhere near, on this border of the forest?

Stung by a sense of neglect, the wizard turned aside from his errand and took a path that brought him out close beside a small log house, sheltered by the mountain to one side, and by the forest at its back. The door stood open and as the wizard approached, a pleasant-faced woman of middle years came out, carrying a bucket. She started at the sight of the stranger, and spilt dirty water onto her own gown.

"I am sorry, my dear." His kindly tone reassured her. "Let me help you."
Soon they were seated comfortably on the wooden bench beside the door, looking out over the pleasant prospect of fields and hedges; there was one very tall tree visible in the field farthest away. The woman brought milk and fruit.

"How may I help you, Sir?" she asked.

"I am seeking some old friends, and I believed they lived here. Can they have moved away, I wonder? Do you know anything of the brothers, Agravin and Montague?"

The woman's face grew sad. "Yes, indeed Sir," she replied, "for they were my own mother's brothers, and I cared for them here until they died. You should have come three years ago, Sir, if you wanted to see my uncle Agravin, and before last winter to see Montague."

The wizard was stunned. "What did they die of?" he cried in horror. "They were so young and vital when last I saw them!"

The woman edged away from him, puzzled.

"They died of old age," she said, eyeing the wizard's broad shoulders and glossy brown hair. "Of old age, Sir. Agravin was near eighty when he died, and Montague well past seventy, though it was hard to tell with him, so cheerful as he was."

Seeing her renewed fear, the wizard hastened to reassure her.

"I had forgotten," he said ruefully, "the speed of Time. Madam, I am the wizard of whom your uncles must surely have spoken, whom they helped so generously many years ago. Alas, I have failed in courtesy to forget them for so long. I hoped to get to know them better; but now their lives have ended."

"Oh, yes, Sir, they have spoken of you so often, especially Montague. Even in the town where I lived before my husband died, folk had heard stories of their dealings with you. Many were afraid, but my mother, that was their only sister, Sir, told me nothing but good could come from them helping you, if you were a good wizard. Which, begging your pardon, Sir, it seems to me you are." For a moment there was a strong look of Montague about her laughing eyes.

"Well!" said the wizard, "I thank you for that, my dear. But what can you tell me of their lives after we met? What was the fate of my two seeds? And what of you? Do you live here alone, so far from company?"

Before answering, she went into the house and quickly returned with a second tray, on which stood a good-sized jug of home-made wine and two goblets. When they were each provided with this refreshment, she began her story.

"My name is Elyn, Sir, and I have lived here for four years. My husband died about then, and as my uncles were both failing it seemed sensible to come to them here. We eased each other's trouble, you might say. And it has been a good place for my boy. I have one son, Sir, born late to me as I was to my own mother, and a great blessing he is to me. He is seven years old now, and his name is Perian. So strong and quick he has grown on the fruit of the tree, and in the quiet country air. We are well content."

"The tree?" the wizard leaned forward. "Was it Agravin's seed that grew into a tree? And planted not far away?"

Elyn pointed. "That is Agravin's tree. And it gives us all we need. No other fruit could do us so much good, I am sure."

"And Montague?" he prompted. "What did he choose to do with his seed?"

Before Elyn could answer a high clear voice broke in.

"He climbed the mountain and planted it on the highest soil in the world and it grew to be the loveliest flower that ever was; but the thorns tore his eye out when he plucked it."

Here the speaker ran out of breath and the wizard, turning, was able to look at him. Perian had appeared around the corner of the house, and stood fearlessly regarding the stranger.

"Well!" said the wizard.

"Oh, Perian, dear!" said Elyn, aware that wizards could be subtle and quick to anger. But this one was smiling.

"Come closer, boy," he said. And Perian did. The two

examined one another silently, then both smiled at once.

"He has a look of both his great-uncles, I think. He has the strength of Agravin and sparkling eyes like Montague's."

"Yes, Sir, he does favour my side of the family, it's true. Though I could wish for more of Agravin in him at times."

"Indeed?" queried the wizard, interested; while Perian fidgeted and said, "Oh, mother!"

"He has some wild notions now and then," she went on, "and too many hours spent listening to Montague and his tales of journeys and mountains and that flower of his; well, it's unsettling, Sir, to a youngster."

"Mmmm," the wizard agreed absently, "it would be, of course. Perian!"

"Sir?"

"I have no seeds left, child. Those were a magic of my youth, and I have different powers now. But what would you desire most in all the world?"

"To climb the mountain," said the boy almost before the wizard had finished speaking, "and look into the heart of the thorn and see the flower, if it can ever grow again. That is what I would like. Sir, please," he added, mindful of his mother's eye on him.

The wizard rose.

"Elyn," he said, "I tell you this; seven years from now, on his fourteenth birthday, Perian should set off up the mountain in search of the thorn. If he has the courage to go, and you the courage to let him, much good may come of it. Do you trust my word?"

"Oh, Mother, please!" cried Perian.

"Well - I don't know..." Elyn looked into the wizard's eyes.

"I'll try, Sir, when the time comes, for you have brought us good in the past, save for uncle Montague's poor eye. I'll try."

"Good; then I must leave you now, with my blessing. Peace be on your house."

"And peace attend your path," they responded. The wizard set off across the fields to resume his interrupted journey.

The years passed quietly, and the only signs of magic in the air were the little silent ones that surrounded Agravin's tree. Perian grew tall and strong and his mother knew in her heart that she could not hope to keep him from the mountain forever. Therefore in her simple wisdom she thought it best to encourage him to go on the day set by the wizard, whose good influence would surely be at work to protect her child.

So on the day he was fourteen, Perian, his knapsack laden with good things - including fruit from the tree – set off up the path to the mountain. He thought his heart would burst with excitement as he turned the corner that led him out of sight of his home for the first time in his life. He remembered to turn and wave to his mother down by the house; but all his impulse was on and upward. "I can never hope to be as happy as this, ever again," he told himself. "This is all my dreams coming true in one adventure."

Spring sunshine and blue skies combined with youth and strength to carry Perian far on his way by nightfall. The journey that used to occupy his uncle Montague for nine, took him only seven days. Rounding a shoulder of the mountain about noon on the seventh day, Perian saw before him the place he had so often heard described. An area of bright green grass, lush soil watered by a gentle spring, and in the midst of all...

Perian gave a cry of horror and fell to his knees, casting up his arms to hide his face. The thorn! The tangled thorn, thick and dark, cast a shadow all about it. How could beauty dwell at its heart? The stricken boy fell on the grass and began to weep, all his trust in uncles and wizards and goodness gone from him in the moment of that fearful vision.

"Perian."

He looked up. The wizard stood before him, anxiety in his face. "Perian. Get up. You had to see. But there is no need for despair. Come, and I will show you a mystery. Only be brave, and all will be well, I promise you."

Perian got up and reluctantly followed him towards the thorn. They stopped beside it and the wizard said:

"You must kneel, and look into the heart of the thorn. Have faith, and courage, and you will see what is to be seen."

Perian looked trembling into the darkness, and there, at its heart, shone the object of all his desire. A single flower glowing in the gloom. It was the colour of a flame; yellow and orange and blue, and it flickered faintly, so that it seemed about to fade away. It was like porcelain and like silk. It seemed eternal and transitory, tantalising and reassuring. Perian's heart was filled with love and anguish.

"Oh!" he cried. "If I could only set you free!"

"Would you repeat Montague's mistake, then?" asked the wizard. "Would you try to wrench the flower from the depths of the thorn?"

Perian thought. "No, not that," he said. "But I would like to find a way to free the flower from the darkness, all the same."

The wizard nodded. He seemed pleased.

"Very well, my boy. Each year from now on you may come here to look at the flower, at about the time of your birthday. I will not be here, but I think you do not fear solitude, with the flower to comfort you?"

Perian shook his head.

"No. But that will not free the flower. Is there nothing I can do to free this beauty from its prison?"

"Yes," said the wizard in a matter-of-fact tone, "of course there is. But will you really want to when you find out how hard it is?"

"I will do anything," said Perian stoutly, his face a perfect blend of Agravin's tenacity and Montague's eagerness. "Anything."

"Look up," said the wizard, "to the high peaks beyond this mountain. Where we stand there is already no trace of snow, but they are greater mountains than this one and their peaks rest ever in the lofty solitude of eternal snow and ice. But in the heart of that cold waste, Perian, there is a miracle to be found."

Perian turned his gaze away from the awful snow-peaks and looked expectantly at the wizard.

"On a high plateau, in the very midst of that desolation, there rises a spring. It runs clear and cold as crystal, unaffected by the freezing wind, for a short distance, and then vanishes again into the mountain. If water from that spring is sprinkled onto the thorn, it will wither away for ever and the flower will be free."

Perian's silence was profound. He looked from the peaks to the thorn and back again.

"Will the flower survive without the protection of the thorn?"

"The thorn does not protect the flower, it is a shadow of evil that seeks to obscure it; and the name of the shadow is fear. If the thorns of fear are withered away, then the light and the scent and the soft music of the flower will be set loose to drift on the wind down into the lands below, and the flower itself will grow taller and stronger. And down in the farmland and in the city the shadows will lessen and burdens will be lighter and hope will be stronger and sorrows diminished, a little. Is it worth the danger, do you think?"

Perian did not see the tension in the wizard's face, his sudden look of age as he waited for his answer. The young man was looking back into the valley, his head to one side as if he were listening.

"Very well, then," he said, and set off so fast that the astonished wizard nearly let him go.

"Wait, Perian, wait! You cannot go yet, you are yet a boy. In seven years you will be ready. Come here on your birthday, bringing food and clothes fit for the hard journey. Then you may set out to find the spring. Go home now and tell your mother all that has happened."

For seven years Perian worked beside his mother on the farm. Each year he would go up the mountain to see the flower and return, refreshed, to tending the two fields and helping Elyn around the house. He learnt of cooking and the uses of herbs, of wine-making and the preserving of fruit for the winter months. Elyn told him stories of her childhood and about his father Kerig. She told him of Lavrum City to the south, of the legend of Verumis and the kings and queens who had followed him. They were very happy together and Perian grew into a fine young man.

Shortly after his twenty-first birthday, Perian stood again before the thorn, a heavy bundle at his feet. His mother had contrived garments of fur and wool, mittens and jerkins and thick heavy coverings for his feet. She had invented a kind of bag for him to sleep in, made of two blankets sewn together with their outer surfaces well oiled to keep off the damp. He had an abundant store of dried fruits and smoked meats and thrice-baked biscuits, together with a bottle of water that he hoped would suffice until he got to where he could gather snow to melt. He was wildly excited and terribly afraid. He wondered for a moment whether his mother wasn't right to wish that he had more of Agravin's prudence in his nature. "Uncle Montague," he muttered, "where are you leading me?"

But kneeling before the flower he found his tranquillity restored, and his conviction that he must carry out his resolve. Looking enraptured into that light, he could see how much good must come of its being set free into the world. He rose and set out over the shoulder of the mountain, heading for the ridge that linked it with the higher peaks he sought. As he went, he whistled, and the startled heights seemed to lean closer to listen.

Nine days later he was past whistling. His lips were cracked and bleeding, his face sore and blistered by the endless freezing wind and the cruel harsh sunlight that reflected from the snow and ice around him. He was cold, so cold that he would have wept tears of self-pity, but that tears froze before they could ease his grief. He was lonely, and tried to talk to himself in his cracked harsh voice, but the bitter air pierced his chest. At night the implacable stars seemed to stare down at him accusingly, so that he tried to hide in his sodden, heavy blanket-bag. He had some food left still, plenty in fact since he could hardly bear the pain of chewing and swallowing. For water he gathered snow into his flask and held it against his body as he walked. He got very little in this way, and was always thirsty. His eyes itched and stung all the time, so that he feared he, like Montague, would pay for his insolent challenge to the shadow of fear, with the loss of sight – perhaps in both eyes. He was frightened, shaking with a fear that never left him.

On the thirteenth day he heard a sound that was not the tortured crying of the wind. He stopped, confused, and tried to focus his aching eyes. So numbed was he that he could hardly take in what he saw. But it was there, in truth. A pure crystal stream sprang laughing in the midst of desolation, and Perian knew again a moment of fierce joy. He stumbled forward and filled his flask with the precious water, stowing it carefully away in his bundle to carry it to the flower. And then horror seized him and he fell weakly to the ground.

"I shall die!" he cried aloud to the heedless wilderness. "How can I get back? This water is not for me to drink, and I have only one flask. I am a fool, and I shall die a fool's death."

And he wept then in earnest, dry and agonising sobs of despair. For all his hope and desire had come to nothing.

But in that black moment light came to him, and it seemed that the endless lamenting of the wind died away. His feet suddenly ceased to feel cold and his eyes to sting. And a voice more gentle than he had ever heard said to him, "Drink, my child, and be refreshed, for you have done what was needed and done it well; shall I not then give you to drink of my fountain?"

Perian looked up into a face he could never afterwards clearly describe. It was most like a woman of great beauty, but whether old or young, fair or dark, he could not say.

Only he saw power and wisdom there, and welling deeps of love in the shining eyes. And fear left him. And he bent and drank from the crystal flow, and was refreshed.

"Now," the voice was saying, "you may drink freely from the flask as you return, for however much you drink it will never be empty. When you have sprinkled the thorn with the final flaskful, however, that will be the last of it. This water could not endure the journey down into the valley."

Perian nodded, too tired to speak. But he smiled and closed his eyes contentedly. Then he felt a light warm touch on his brow and heard the voice saying, "Peace attend your path." When he opened his eyes again, he was alone. He got to his feet, and set off almost jauntily to retrace his steps. He whistled into the teeth of the rising wind.

Only half the time was consumed on the return journey that had been needed for the ascent. Perian felt almost strong enough to fly. He ate nothing at all, and the more he depended entirely on the miraculous water for sustenance, the stronger he became. He reached the flower a week after his encounter by the spring. Trembling with eagerness, he shed his pack and brought out the precious flask. Stepping up to the thorn, he sprinkled the water onto as many branches as he could reach. For a tortured moment nothing happened. Then suddenly the whole thicket seemed to boil away in a black vapour, so that Perian cried out in fear that the flower would be destroyed. But the vapour cleared as rapidly as it had come, and the flower stood revealed to the light of day. Perian knelt before it, and watched in wonder as it grew, as its light intensified, as a sweetness of music and perfume wafted around him and away into the rejoicing air. He knelt for hours before he was startled out of his absorption by the voice of the wizard behind him.

"Well, Perian - so with Agravin's strength you have at last

carried out Montague's vision. How does it feel?"

"Good," replied Perian, "very good."

"Then shall we go now, and gladden your poor mother's heart with the sight of you? Besides, I feel it would be a great pleasure to taste again that good wine made from the fruit of Agravin's tree."

And so they set off together down the mountain.

A week later Perian and the wizard arrived back at Two Fields Farm. Perian was looking tired but elated and the wizard was obviously in good humour. Elyn kissed Perian and clasped the wizard's hand.

"Sit down and I'll get you something to eat. You both look as though you need it."

For several days Perian was glad to do little more than rest and eat and talk about his journey. The wizard stayed and helped Elyn care for her son, using his knowledge of herbs and medicines to restore Perian's strength.

Before long Perian was fully recovered and one morning the wizard took him to one side.

"I must leave you today, but before I go I must talk to you. I will set out after we have eaten. Will you walk with me a little way, then we can talk as we go along?"

Perian agreed, and after a small feast, farewells and thanks were exchanged with Elyn, and Perian and the wizard set off towards Skalwood. When they reached the edge of the forest the wizard stopped.

"Now you have released the flower, do you think that everything has been achieved? Is there more to be done?"

"I suppose there is more, but l don't know what."

"I will tell you this. None of us knows the destination before we take the first step."

"But what is the first step?"

"That is for you to decide. I will go now. Peace be on your house, Perian."

Perian frowned before replying:

"Peace attend your path."

Then the wizard entered the forest and Perian went to his mother, and told her what the wizard had said.

"I do not understand. Mother, and he did not want to say more or speak more plainly. Can you tell me what this means?"

She paused and took a deep breath.

"This time has to come to every mother and every son. The meaning of his words is plain. It is time for you to go and find your place in the world. It is time for you to leave me and seek your fate: I fear yours is a hard one."

"I would not leave you, mother. Who would chop the wood and tend the tree?"

Elyn reached out and took Perian's hand. She smiled. 'I am not so old, yet, that I cannot chop a few logs, and the tree needs little tending. The wizard told you. It is time to go, and you must go. I would have you stay, but you must go."

"But where should I go, Mother, and what should I take with me?"

"You must choose the way: the wizard said that. And you will take my love with you, and the rest you will find along the way, I think."

The next day, early in the morning, Perian set off, taking some bread, some fruit of the tree and a flask of water in a pack on his back. He carried a stout staff of ash wood. His mother stood at the cottage door and waved until he reached the top of a hill. There he stopped, waved back and then continued down the other side and was lost to view.

3 Skalwood

Once out of sight of home, Perian remembered his last journey and a feeling of excitement and vitality arose within him.

"That was hard," he said to himself, "but at least I knew where I was going." He stopped and thought for a moment.

"Well, I have seen the cold mountain-tops, so now I should go to the warm valley and the great river Siannen that runs down to the sea. Perhaps I will come to Lavrum City."

The decision cheered him and he set off again at a good pace.

This is a bit easier, he thought, and at least it is downhill.

When he had walked over a low ridge and topped the hill beyond it he saw the forest, spread out before him like a green sea. A mist was rising from the mass of trees and he could not see the far side sloping down into the valley. He went forward eagerly. He had never been far into the forest, and he looked curiously at the plants and the signs of animals. He had learnt from Montague how to distinguish the tracks of deer from those of wild pigs, how to tell where a fox had passed or a stoat had hunted. Looking beneath the trees for the hidden forest flowers, he was sometimes startled by a chattering noise above his head, as squirrels sprang from branch to branch and tree to tree.

Before long he realised that he was well into the forest.

He looked back and saw that the light of the open country was shut out by tree trunks and looking up he could see only small patches of sky through the roof of branches and leaves. Evening was falling and the mist was swirling between the trees. Perian suddenly felt cold and set about making a fire. He warmed himself and ate a little food, then fell asleep as the fire burned and the light faded. He was woken at dawn by the noises of the forest and continued his journey. As the morning went on he passed deeper into the forest. The sun was rising higher in the sky above the green canopy, but little light penetrated to the forest floor. Perian was beginning to wonder how to avoid getting lost without the sun to guide him, when he saw the light of a clearing ahead of him and to his right. As he neared the break in the forest he heard sounds of scuffling and shouting coming from the open space. When he emerged from the trees he saw what was causing the noise.

There were three men trying to gain control of a horse. It was a magnificent black stallion, proud and stately, and not to be mastered easily. It had three ropes tied about its neck and there was a man hanging on the end of each rope. As Perian watched, the horse dragged the men around the clearing on their stomachs. If one got to his feet, the horse would change direction and the man would fall over again. The sight of the men standing up, staggering about, tripping over each other and the ropes, falling down backwards and forwards and all the time shouting instructions to each other, kept Perian amused for quite a while.

Eventually he took pity on them, went forward and called, "Hello there, can I help?"

The three men stopped and looked towards him and were immediately toppled once more by the horse. One of them shouted to Perian from the ground:

"Yes, if you think you can."

"This animal is upset and frightened," said Perian as he approached the horse. 'I will try to calm him while you hold the ropes."

He walked slowly towards the wild-eyed animal and it backed away from him warily.

"What is his name?" he said, keeping his eyes on the horse.

"Garren," said one of the men.

Perian concentrated on the tall stallion.

"Hush, Garren, noble beast," Perian said quietly as he advanced. Garren lowered his head and turned towards Perian.

As he did so the grooms pulled the ropes tight about his neck and he lifted his head again and started to pull away.

"No, let the ropes go slack," said Perian in a commanding tone. The men stopped pulling the ropes and the horse seemed to relax.

The clearing was now perfectly quiet and Perian was an arm's length away from Garren's proud head: he stopped and, looking into the horse's eyes, spoke quietly:

"Hush, noble Garren. Be my friend and I will be yours."

Garren moved forward and rubbed his nose against Perian's chest. Perian smiled.

The three grooms started to move towards the horse but stopped when he lifted his head to look at them. Perian removed two of the ropes from Garren's neck and tied the third to a sapling. The horse started cropping the grass.

"Thank you, young man," said the oldest of the grooms. "I don't know what got into the animal. We have been travelling for four days without any trouble, but this morning he starts playing up. My name is Craigan, chief groom to Marannan, horse-master of Lassian, and these are my assistants Hrinan and Therior."

"I am Perian. I was travelling to the river, perhaps to Lavrum, though I do not know the way."

"To Lavrum? The way is simple enough in the telling. South to the Siannen, then follow it eastwards. But perhaps we can be travelling companions. In any case it is close to mid-day, will you share our food?"

As they sat in the clearing, Perian told the grooms of his life on the farm with his mother and of his journey. Hrinan and Therior hardly said a word but Craigan told of Lassian and the stables of Marannan.

"We are taking this horse to the king at Lavrum. Every ten years or so our master, the greatest horse-master in the world, sends his best animal for the king's use. It is said that any king may have a crown, but the king at Lavrum must have a Lassian steed."

"He is indeed worthy of a king," said Perian, looking once more at the horse quietly munching grass, "but, excuse me for saying so, he seems to need more training."

"I see what you mean, after this morning's events," said the groom, "but he really is fully trained to the bit and I wonder if there is something in the forest hereabouts upsetting him; wolves or bears perhaps. But we have seen none, nor any trace of wild beasts. I hoped that you would travel with us as you seem to have a gift for dealing with horses."

Perian laughed at that.

"Yes, I think you are right, but I cannot imagine why that should be, since I have hardly even seen one before. But I will gladly come with you if I can be of help."

When they had finished eating, Perian took up his bag and staff, Hrinan and Therior tied a large pack onto Garren's back and Craigan made to lead him. But as he approached, the horse shied away. Craigan withdrew and spoke to Perian.

"Would you try to lead him, he seems to have taken a dislike to me."

Perian went forward and untied the halter from the sapling. The black stallion allowed himself to be led out of the glade. The grooms followed at a distance: if they tried to catch up, Garren would walk faster or stop and advance on them until they withdrew. Eventually, Perian lost sight of them altogether. He stopped Garren and went back to look for them, but he could not find them. As darkness was falling, he decided to make camp and hoped that they would catch up with him in the morning. But morning came and there was no sign of the men of Lassian.

"It seems that I must finish their task for them. They must have missed me in the dark. I will meet them again at Lavrum, if not before, for they cannot return to their master and report that they have lost the king's mount."

After finishing his simple breakfast he set out again with Garren walking quietly at his side. As he walked he talked to the horse about the things he saw. He pointed out flowers that he knew and made up names for those that were new to him. They stopped occasionally to admire some great ancient tree or flowering bush. It seemed to Perian that Garren was listening attentively to all he said and sometimes he half expected the horse to add some comment of his own.

The morning passed pleasantly in this way until, emerging from some undergrowth, they came suddenly upon a strange scene. There was a large outcrop of rock blocking their path and seated at its base were two men staring mournfully at a litter bearing what appeared to be a knight in armour. Perian thought they must be two squires and their dead or wounded master. They did not seem to notice his approach.

"I hesitate to intrude upon your grief," he said when he was quite close to them. They started from their reverie and looked him up and down. Then they looked at Garren approvingly.

"I beg your pardon?" said one.

"I am sorry to disturb you in your sorrow, but I have not met so many people in this wood that I could pass you by."

"Sorrow?" The same man spoke, looking bewildered.

"Is your master not wounded or worse? I thought from your sad faces..."

Perian was interrupted by the laughter of the two men. He was taken aback by their strange behaviour.

"I'm sorry, I'm sorry," said the second man through his laughter, "but this is not our master." He pointed to the litter. "It is merely a suit of armour."

There was a pause while Perian tried to understand what had been said. He looked at the finely crafted armour, decorated in silver and white. Then he too laughed.

"I'm sorry," he said, abashed. "You must think me very foolish. But you looked so sad sitting there that I thought..."

"That's all right," said the first man, smiling, "but our sadness is well-founded. We are to take this armour to Lavrum for the king, but my friend Bannig here has broken his leg. And when he fell the litter broke too. We are unable to go on. I cannot take Bannig back home and leave the armour here, nor can I go for help and leave him here to be eaten by wolves. What are we to do?"

Perian thought for a moment, then spoke.

"It is good fortune that has brought me this way, for I can surely help you. I am taking this horse to Lavrum for the king. Garren could carry the armour and your friend."

"Thank you," said Bannig, "but I fear I could not ride a horse, for my leg gives me great pain. Perhaps you and Theyrig could take the armour while I wait here for his return. Even if I were to be helped we would take too long,"

"No, I will not leave you here in the forest alone, Bannig, it is too dangerous!" exclaimed Theyrig.

"Well, what can we do?" asked Perian. "If you would trust me I could take the armour with the horse and you could help Bannig to some aid."

"We accept your offer, young man."

"Good," said Perian, "I am glad I can be of help and I promise to present the suit to the king as soon as possible."

With that the three men took food together. Then the armour was loaded onto Garren's strong back and Perian went on his way.

He travelled for the rest of the day, going gradually downhill all the time. The trees were closer together now and finding a path was increasingly difficult. Garren seemed able to find ways through the thicket whenever Perian was undecided, but the horse had difficulty moving past the branches that stretched across their path and caught in the bundles tied to his back. Perian forced a way through, using his staff to lever and beat the branches out of the way. Long before the sun went down, progress became impossible as neither man nor horse could see the way forward. As the darkness deepened, Perian could hear the rustling sounds of large animals hunting in the thickets around him, and the cries of the small creatures that fell victim to them. An owl flew out in front of the travellers and startled Garren. By the time Perian had quietened him, it was time to make camp for the night.

In the morning they pressed on, refreshed, and seemed to make better progress. Eventually the path became clearer and Perian could see more light in the distance. "I think we will soon be at the edge of the forest, my friend."

The horse stopped walking. Perian turned to him in surprise. "What's wrong, Garren? Would you rather stay in the dark forest?"

Garren lifted his head and started pulling back against the halter. Something was upsetting him and Perian turned to peer into the tangle ahead of them. As he did so a young lad leapt into his path bearing a shield and a sword, both of which were too big for him.

"Stop and pay homage to the king!" shouted the boy, waving the sword about his head with difficulty and peering over the top of the shield.

"Gladly," said Perian, "where is he?"

"Where is he!" the boy sneered. "He is before you. You are before him. I am the king."

Perian could not stop himself from laughing, even though he was in grave danger from the flailing sword.

"What are you laughing at, peasant?" demanded the boy angrily, resting his sword for a moment. "Have you ever seen the king?"

"No."

"Do you know his name?"

"No."

"Then how do you know I am not the king?"

Perian bowed low.

"I am sorry. Your Majesty. I was misled by your dirty face, your ragged clothes, your rudeness and the smell that alerted this horse to your presence. Your Majesty."

"You're making fun of me!" shouted the boy. "I am the king! This is the royal shield bearing the Flaming Flower of the House of Lavrum and this is Sheean made for the hand of the king." He wielded the sword once more, this time cutting a thick branch from a tree with one stroke.

"Please be careful with that blade," said Perian, "or you will do yourself an injury. If, as you say, that sword was made for the hand of the king, then you are certainly not he, for it belongs in your hand as much as a plough belongs on a platter. Now tell me who you are."

"I am Bryn, the chief apprentice of Jurth the swordsmith, and I am good enough to best you in combat!"

He charged at Perian with a cry of rage. He nearly tripped over the shield as he came and Perian easily sidestepped the wild swing of the sword and brought his staff down onto the boy's unprotected sword-arm. Bryn dropped the sword and ran off the way he had come, discarding the shield as he went. Aware how close he had been to death, Perian stood and watched the boy make his escape. Even in the hands of an artless boy, Sheean was a dangerous weapon. Perian picked up the sword and weighed it in his hand. It was beautifully made and although it was quite heavy its perfect balance made it seem as light as the wooden sword he had had as a boy. He walked over to the shield and picked it up, peering into the undergrowth where the boy had disappeared to make sure that there was no further danger. A metallic glint caught his eye and he discovered a scabbard and belt of white leather, decorated with silver and bearing the same flower symbol as the shield. The sword slid into its scabbard smoothly and Perian took it and the shield and added them to the load on Garren's back. "More gifts for the king," he whispered to the horse, and they walked together towards the light.

Soon they reached the edge of the forest and Perian looked out over the open land. He could see rich farm fields spread out before him, and in the distance the broad river. They walked across some pastures where cows were grazing and came to a narrow lane between high hedges. Perian stopped to think, then spoke to Garren.

"If we always go downhill, we will come to the river Siannen. Then we can follow it to Lavrum."

It was a mild day and strolling along the lane in daylight was a pleasant contrast to walking in the dark wood. They met no-one: the countryside seemed deserted, except for the farm animals they heard from time to time through the hedges.

By evening they were close to the river and the lane broadened until it met a wide, open road running alongside the slow-moving water. They stopped and looked at the Siannen.

"I travelled up this same river when I was young, but further to the west." Perian pointed and the horse seemed to nod his understanding. "But we must go downstream to Lavrum. Let's walk that way for a while and then make camp on the bank."

They walked together as the sun set behind them until Garren checked, sniffing the air. Perian, alerted, smelt the smoke from a fire and something cooking, and as he went forward he saw a figure silhouetted against the river, tending some fish spitted over a small fire.

The cook did not take any notice of their approach.

"Hello there," called Perian. The man looked up, his face showing neither pleasure nor anxiety.

"Hello, young man. Will you join me for supper?"

"Yes please; it smells wonderful." Perian removed the packs from Garren's back and set him to graze on the lush riverbank. The stranger was concentrating on his cooking. Then he called to Perian,

"They're ready now. Come and eat. I'm afraid I have only one plate; I hadn't expected guests." He handed Perian a skewer with three fish on it, took another for himself and they both ate, watching the last light fade from the sky.

When they had finished, the stranger produced a bottle of wine, opened it, drank a mouthful and handed it to Perian.

"And who is my guest?"

"My name is Perian and I am travelling to Lavrum."

"That is a fine horse. Lassian, isn't it?"

"Yes, how did you know?"

"Had one like it myself once. Did you steal it?"

Perian was taken aback by the blunt question. "No! I did not!" He started to rise.

"Sit down. Sit down. I will apologise for my insult if you will tell me how you came by that beast. It must be a remarkable story, for you did not trade it for five sacks of potatoes, nor even fifty."

"It is quite simple," said Perian, "it is not my horse. I am taking it to the king in Lavrum." And Perian told the stranger of his journey through Skalwood.

"I knew it would be a strange story," said the older man, "though it's not the strangest that ever came out of Skalwood. But I have not introduced myself. I am Angorian. And I must tell you that you will not find the king in Lavrum, for he is not there. He has abdicated and Lavrum is governed by the Council of Advice."

Perian looked worried.

"What should I do, then? Take the armour, and sword, and Garren, to the Council?"

"Why not take another drink from the bottle and pass it to me and leave decisions till the morning? Would you like to know why there is no king in Lavrum?"

Perian passed the bottle.

"Yes. It does seem odd."

"The short answer is that he is at this moment seated on the banks of the River Siannen sharing a bottle of wine with a young traveller called Perian."

Perian sat up with a look of horror.

"My lord! I had no idea!"

"No, no, sit down. I am no longer king and the ceremony of court is out of place here. Have another drink and I will tell you something few people know."

He passed Perian the bottle again.

"Well, since you do not even know your king's name you will not have heard of the adventures of my youth: how I travelled up the Old North Road through the mountains to where people have long feet and slide around the snow on them: or how I travelled to the west where there is no sea, and saw the ancient city of Saracoma and walked its dead and deserted streets." The old king's eyes laughed at the memories. Perian moved closer to the fire, and he too remembered.

"I heard such tales when I was a boy, but I thought they were just stories for children, like the ones about bears that eat porridge and dragons that hoard gold."

"I think you should remember that every story is told for a reason. Often there is more truth in fables than in the decrees of kings. But I daresay the story-tellers have made my deeds more glorious than they were. All that was long ago in my youth, when I was strong and foolish. For years now, I have stayed in Lavrum City and tried to rule wisely, to keep this a peaceful and prosperous land. All very dull!" Angorian burst out laughing and took another drink from the bottle.

"But no; it was not dull. When I was as young as you, I would have thought it so. But there was Lastra, my Queen, and Alauda my beautiful strong daughter. Life could not be dull while they breathed the air of Lavrum."

He paused and looked into the fire. As the light flickered over his face, he suddenly looked old.

"But Lastra died last spring, just when the early flowers were coming out. And Alauda is gone, too.

"I had no heart for ruling without my Queen. I decided I would leave the care of the realm to Princess Alauda and pass my last years in private pursuits, as is the custom. I thought I might journey in Skalwood and seek out its mysteries. But my duties could not be cast aside so easily: for by the ancient custom of Lavrum, the heir to the throne, whether man or woman, must choose a consort before the coronation. So Alauda set out with a small company to search throughout the realm. First she went westwards and then she was to return and visit the islands to the east. But she has not returned, and three days ago a rumour came from Skalbyrg that she was lost and that wickedness was the cause. Now I travel there alone to find out the truth of the matter."

"But why have you not brought a company of men to help you in your search? It takes four eyes to look four ways, so surely two hundred would be better than two."

Angorian nodded at the question.

"Yes, I've wondered about that, but I had a strong feeling that one pair of eyes would be better, that I would see more from the ground than on horseback and that I would move faster without the weight of a crown on my head. So you see a simple traveller going to Skalbyrg. Few will recognise a king without his trappings and trumpets."

"So, you are in disguise?"

"Well, I do not want a herald going before me to announce my coming: the doers of evil are watchful and I must try to catch them unawares. Will you help me in this, though it is not your fight? It may prove to be a wild goose chase, but it might be an adventure worth a young man's trouble."

Perian's eyes lit up.

"It would be an honour, my lord! But I fear I would be of little use to you: more of a hindrance than a help. And besides I have promised to take these things to Lavrum."

"Ah yes; the royal arms and armour. They could prove very useful. Though I am not now the king, I think I can release you from your promise. You have delivered your burdens to me, and I have a use for them in my quest, if you will agree to help me."

"Who am I to refuse the request of a king? I will gladly do your bidding." There was little reluctance in Perian's manner.

"Thank you, young Perian. We will discuss it further in the morning. Now let us get some sleep."

They settled down, one on each side of the fire, and slept soundly till dawn, while Garren watched over them.

4   To Waslant

The old king and Perian talked as they ate their breakfast.

"I have an idea," said Angorian, "but before I tell you about it I would like to see if you can ride that horse."

They opened the packages that Garren had been carrying and discovered a white saddle and harness, beautifully made, and decorated with silver flowers. The black stallion looked truly regal with the white and silver fittings and Perian hesitated to mount him.

"Go on, Perian. If he will let you mount then you are fit to ride him."

Perian murmured a few words into Garren's ear, then swung into the saddle. The horse stood quite still, calmly waiting.

"I have little knowledge of horsemanship, my lord. But Garren and I are friends and I think he will help me."

Perian took hold of the reins, spoke to the horse and rode at a walk around the old king. After two circuits he spoke again and Garren halted.

"You sit well, Perian, and you understand your horse. The rest will come in time. Good. Now dismount and try this armour for size."

Perian looked puzzled at this request, but did as he was asked. The armour fitted him well and was light to wear.

"Now sit upon Garren again."

Perian mounted and Angorian walked round the horse looking at them from every direction.

"Good. Excellent. Now get down again and take the armour off. I'll have to cut your hair to a more courtly style, and you must have a good wash, but with a clean shirt you will pass for a prince or a knight quite easily."

Perian started to remove the armour.

"I do not understand, my lord. You said that you wished to travel unknown, but these beautiful things will surely attract attention."

"Yes, they will attract attention to you and away from me. If there are wrongdoers around Skalbyrg they will be expecting someone to seek the princess and they will be ready to put obstacles in your way, but who will take notice of an old squire called . . . what shall it be? Gorig. Who will care about old Gorig the faithful servant? And while they watch you, I will watch them. It may mean some danger for you. Do you still wish to help me?"

"Oh, gladly, my lord!"

"Good. But from now on you must call me Gorig and I will call you 'my lord'. What name should you use?"

"Why not Perian'? It is as good a name as any."

"Yes it is. Very well, my lord Perian, and since you bear the arms of Lavrum, you must be in the service of the Council of Advice. Now hop into the river and we'll give you a good wash and trim your hair."

Perian was washed and scrubbed, his hair was trimmed and he put the armour on again. He mounted Garren and set off for Skalbyrg with the old king walking beside him. As they went Angorian instructed Perian in how to play his part.

That evening a young knight rode into the town with an old servant at his stirrup. They stopped when they reached the large inn at its centre. In the open space in front of The Sentinel's Rest some market-traders were clearing up their goods as the sun went down and the warm lights of the tap-room invited the travellers in.

Angorian set about stabling the horse and Perian entered the warm tap-room and sat down alone at one of the scrubbed wooden tables, in a corner by a flight of stairs leading to an upper floor. He looked around the room and smiled at anyone whose eye he caught. He had never seen so many people collected in one place. There were small groups of men seated round other tables who glanced curiously at the newcomer, but most of them avoided his eye as much as possible. The exception was a small thin man wearing an apron, who looked at Perian squarely, almost aggressively. He left the group of card-players he had been watching and approached Perian.

"Good evening, sir. I am Belryn, the keeper of this hostel. Is there any way I might serve you? There is a pig roasting: it should be ready soon. Or some ale?"

"Yes. Ale please. I will eat later. A room for the night for myself and my man and stabling for my horse."

"Very good, young sir. You'll be from Lavrum?"

"That's right. I have a commission from the Council of Advice."

The inn-keeper did not look impressed, but he stepped back and his face went blank. As he turned to get the drink Perian just heard him mutter, "No trouble here."

Perian sat alone drinking his ale and watching the other men in the room. The only female presence was a young serving girl who occasionally brought a plate of food from the back of the inn. A steady trickle of customers came in while Perian ate his supper and by the time he had finished eating the place was quite crowded and noisy. There were games of cards and dice. There was talk and laughter, argument and spilt drink. Perian was, for the most part, ignored, though each newcomer would look at him curiously before joining one of the noisy groups. No-one, apart from the landlord, spoke to him.

When Perian's meal had been cleared away he stood up. This attracted some attention from nearby tables, but as he moved towards the centre of the room most people took little notice. Only the landlord watched him warily. When Perian reached the middle of the noisy room he found an empty chair, stood on it, and waited. Those nearest to him stopped what they were doing and turned to look at him. A few humorous remarks were made, but eventually the whole room became quiet and all eyes were on the young knight in his richly-decorated armour.

"Thank you for your attention. I need the answer to a question."

He paused and looked round at the blank faces. The only sound to be heard came from the kitchen: the faint noises of cooking and cleaning. Perian continued.

"I have been sent from Lavrum with a commission from the Council of Advice concerning the Princess Alauda, our Queen-to-be. Some time ago she came this way to see her people and how they fared. But she has not returned. I seek news of her. My question is: do you know where the Princess Alauda is?"

The men of Skalbyrg murmured amongst themselves, but nobody seemed prepared to give Perian an answer. He waited a while before speaking again. Now his manner was more commanding.

"Will nobody help me? The throne of Lavrum is empty and she who should occupy it may be in danger. Will you sit there muttering all night while I await an answer?"

The room became quiet again but nobody seemed willing to speak up. Perian said nothing. He stood quite still, and waited. Finally Belryn the inn-keeper stepped forward.

"We know nothing, young lord. The princess was here, but she did not stay long. She went to the west. We know nothing."

Perian stared into Belryn's eyes, then looked round the room to see the men nodding their agreement. He looked at the inn-keeper again.

"That is all you can tell me?"

"We know nothing more."

"Well, thank you all, for your help." Perian smiled, stepped down from the chair and went back to his table. He was brought a mug of ale and as he sat drinking it he again watched the men talking and carrying on with their games. The room seemed quieter than before and no-one looked towards him. He finished his drink and asked Belryn where his room was. As he went up the stairs the noises of dice, laughter and drinking grew louder.

The room was small and poorly furnished but clean. Angorian was sitting on one of the beds when Perian entered. The old king closed the door and put a ringer to his lips.

"We must talk quietly. I fear there are too many people interested in our doings here. First, at the end of the corridor there is a door to the outside. Steps lead down into the stable-yard. Your horse is in the stall to the left; I have left him saddled, just in case."

"Do you think we are in danger?"

"We may be. There is an unpleasant feeling here. If no attempt is made to hinder us tonight, it may be made on the road. So it would be wise to depart early and quietly. Still, what have you learnt from the good men of Skalbyrg?"

"They say the princess travelled to the west."

"Do they? Then they are lying, for that is not what they believe. Nobody seems certain, but in the kitchen they think she is a captive in Waslant."

"Thorns and thieves."

"That's right. 'Nothing grows in Waslant but thorns and thieves.' There is a gap in the hills to the south of here. Raiders used to come through it to rob and burn in the valley. Skalbyrg was a stronghold in those days, protecting the whole valley. But there have been no raids in my time, nor for many years before. Could they have started again?"

Before Perian could speak, the door opened and Belryn crept into the room.

"I can answer that."

Perian and Angorian jumped up, but the inn-keeper put a finger to his lips.

"I shouldn't be here; it's as much as my life is worth. But maybe you can help. You mustn't mind the men. They're good folk mostly, but they don't have a choice."

Angorian forgot that he was a servant and took charge at once.

"What are you talking about? Have the raids started again?"

"No, not raids. But the dark lady of the desert has been here. She took all our women-folk, excepting the youngest. And when she took them, she took the princess too. From now on we must do whatever she says or they will be lost to us. The men below are afraid she will be angry if we speak of this to you or to any strangers, and will hurt or kill our women."

"Where has she taken them?"

"To the south, into Waslant, that's all I know. I must go before I'm missed."

He slipped quietly out of the room and left Perian and Angorian looking at each other.

Suddenly there was a loud crash and the door burst inwards. Four large men rushed into the room but once inside they stopped. Three of them carried large kitchen knives and one had a rusty sword. Before they had advanced two paces, Perian had Sheean in his hand. The sight of the pale glow of its polished blade stopped the intruders for a moment. Angorian had produced a long lethal-looking knife from somewhere and stood beside Perian. He laughed.

"Come. Don't be shy. You wish to die? I think we can oblige you."

With that he leapt forward and plunged his knife into one of the assassins. Perian moved forward but had difficulty using his sword in the small room, and several blows glanced off his armour before he could get a clear swing. When he finally swept Sheean forward his opponent was dead before falling to the floor. He struck a second down as easily then saw the king grappling with the man he had wounded while the one with the sword had somehow got behind him. Perian saw the rusty blade come down on the king's unprotected head. Swiftly Sheean severed the head of the killer and its point sank into the wounded man's chest. Perian would have struck again but the man's eyes glazed over and he fell to the floor, dead.

Perian moved Angorian from the bloody floor to a bed and tried to stop the bleeding from his head. The old king could still speak.

"A good fight. Careless. The armour, the horse, the sword. Yours now. The south, Perian. Alauda. Go!"

Angorian, his body tense, stared into the young man's eyes.

Perian wept as he looked at the king.

"Yes, my lord. To the south."

Only then did the king of Lavrum sink back into the bed and die.

There were shouts coming from elsewhere in the inn. Perian quickly picked up packs, helmet and sword, went along the corridor, through the door and down the steps to the stable. He mounted Garren and rode swiftly and quietly into the dark night.

There was no moon and no starlight. Once Perian had left the town he could not see the road ahead and had to let Garren find the way. Perian listened intently for some sound of pursuit, but could hear nothing but Garren's hooves on the road. They travelled southwards, climbing up towards the Raider's Gap. When they reached the level ground of the pass, Perian brought Garren to a standstill.

"Well, my friend, if we carry on much further we will miss our path, and no-one will find us in this blackness. We might as well get off the road and rest. We will travel faster in the morning."

He dismounted and led the horse off the road. He walked through short grass, feeling his way, until he sensed, rather than saw, that he was near a tree or large bush. They passed through a screen of branches and stopped.

"We should be out of sight of the road, here. And we will hear anybody approaching. But we'd better not light a fire."

Perian wrapped himself in a blanket and settled down on the

soft earth. Soon he was asleep.

It was still dark when he woke, suddenly alert. He could hear Garren beside him breathing evenly, and he concentrated his attention on the sounds from the direction of the road. At first, only the sound of the leaves gently rustling in a light breeze came to him. Then there was a faint whisper of something moving over the grass.

Perian put his hand to the hilt of Sheean and waited, not daring to move. The sound came closer. The branches that shielded Perian's camp stirred and a dim glow appeared beneath the tree. Perian leapt to his feet and drew his sword.

"Stop there, if you value your life!" he shouted.

A quiet voice came from the direction of the light.

"So; now my little Perian is a brave knight and a killer of men. Master your fear and I will reveal myself."

The light grew until beneath the tree it was as bright as day. Perian drew back towards the shadows at the edge. Before him stood the wizard, who gazed sombrely at the agitated young man.

"Do not worry. My light cannot be seen beyond this tree. It is not many days since we last met, but you have changed. Now distrust and death are in your eyes."

"Yes, I have killed and I have seen a friend die through treachery. And I have seen fear and dishonesty, and ignoble people assailing the noble."

The wizard looked sadly at Perian.

"I know. But I have pursued you with a purpose. I went to your home but you had gone. I had not expected you to go so soon."

Perian interrupted eagerly.

"Have you seen my mother? How is she?"

"She is well. Anxious about you, and she asked me to watch over you. I cannot do that, of course, but I should give you one protection in your undertaking. It's the best I can do for you. Your enemy in Waslant will be illusion. Your defence will be reality. Hold onto this and use it in your time of despair. That will be when the enemy is closest. Her true name is Kemara. You will not recognize her for she changes her form, but when she is near, you will know because there will be a feeling of emptiness in your soul and your strength will drain away. Speak her true name and your vision will clear. But do not try to command her; you have not that power. Now sleep."

The light went out suddenly and the wizard was gone. Perian peered into the surrounding darkness and listened. Garren pricked his ears up and stood perfectly still. Nothing could be seen and the only sound was the rustling of leaves. The two companions settled down again to sleep.

They awoke as the sun rose. Perian peered out from the shelter of the branches at the countryside. He was in the shelter of a large apple tree at the north end of Raider's Gap. There was a spring close by, and Perian took a drink from it and looked down into the valley. The course of the Siannen was marked by a mist that hid Skalbyrg from sight. He could see the smoke rising up into the grey morning: the townspeople of Skalbyrg were cooking their breakfasts. To the south was the pass through the hills and the road that led to Waslant. Perian filled his flask with water from the spring.

"We'd better be going before the mist rises or we might have some vengeful Skalbyrgers after us."

The contrast with the green valley of the Siannen could

hardly have been greater. The afternoon sun beat down on a dry brown land sparsely covered by scrubby thorn bushes. The land gradually rose to the south-west, and to the east, through the heat-haze, Perian could dimly see a range of hills.

"South, the king said."

Garren moved forward at a steady pace and Perian let him pick his own way through the brush, always keeping his shadow on his left. There was no wind, and heat came from the clear sky above and the dry land all around. They travelled southwards all afternoon until the sun had moved down to touch the horizon and the sky had changed from white to purple. They camped for the night and rode all the next day in the glare of the sun. As evening was falling on the second day, Garren stopped and Perian looked all around him. He could see no landmark, nor was one place better for a camp than another. He was about to dismount when he felt Garren stiffen. Perian stood up in his stirrups and peered towards the south. There seemed to be someone in the distance moving towards them over the long shadows of the thorns. Perian put on his helmet and took up his shield. He sat and watched the figure approaching. Only when the stranger was quite close did his size become apparent: standing, he was as tall as Perian mounted. He stopped a short distance away, blocking the path, and Perian looked straight into his black eyes as darkness was falling.

The giant figure grinned like a crocodile.

"Go away, little knight, you are not needed here. Go back to your green valley and the sages of Lavrum will praise your courage in coming here and your wisdom in leaving well alone."

Perian drew his sword.

"I have not come in search of praise. Where is the Princess

Alauda?"

The giant laughed.

"Oh please don't threaten me! I get so frightened of sharp things."

Perian spurred Garren forward and Sheean cut through the air towards the giant's head. But as it made contact the giant disappeared and his laughter echoed across the sky like thunder. Garren reared up, his front hooves striking at the space where the giant had been. Perian reined in his horse and looked wildly round.

"Bravely done, young Perian!"

The voice came from behind him. He turned Garren and peered into the darkness. A few paces away he could see two figures dimly lit by a campfire. He rode slowly towards them.

"Come down and join us. The night will be cold before long."

There were two old men seated by the fire. One was small and wiry with a black eye-patch, the other was large and heavy. Both smiled as Perian dismounted and walked towards them.

"Who's there? Who are you?"

The small man turned to the large one.

"Well, brother, who would have thought it? He doesn't know his old uncles."

They both laughed gently.

"My uncles! Montague. Agravin. What are you doing here? You're dead!"

The larger man spoke slowly.

"Well yes, little Perian, we are dead. But that couldn't stop us when you need help."

"No. That couldn't stop us," echoed the other. "Come and sit down."

Perian stayed where he was.

"So far from home, nephew. Your mother is worried about you, you know. Isn't she, Agravin?"

"Oh yes, brother, very worried."

Perian made no reply.

"And what are you doing here? On some adventure?"

"Yes, I'm looking for Princess Alauda of Lavrum."

"A princess! Well, now. I shouldn't think a princess would be here, would you, Agravin?"

"No, not here, brother."

"You've done your best. Perian lad, but I would go home now if I were you. Don't you agree, Agravin?"

"I'd go home, brother, if I were him. You know, nephew, Montague always loved an adventure. And he thinks you should go home. Your mother needs you. Doesn't she, brother?"

"She's not as young as she used to be. She could do with some strong young arms to help."

Perian stepped forward angrily and stood in the firelight looking down at the two old men.

"What are you? You are not my uncles! You have their voices and their faces, but your words are false. I have given my promise to seek the princess. My uncles would not want me to break my word. Let me see you as you are!"

He picked up a burning stick from the fire and held it up as a torch. The stick burst into a bright white light that blinded him with its brilliance. When he could see again, the men, the fire and even the stick in his hand had disappeared and the night was dark and empty.

He went to Garren and stroked the horse's smooth black neck.

"Ah, there you are!"

Perian turned round and his face lit up with recognition and relief. A pale glow stood out against the blackness of the night. Within it stood two human shapes.

"Angorian!"

"Yes, my boy, and let me present you to my beautiful queen. Come closer."

But Perian drew back against Garren's flank and stared at the royal couple.

"But the queen is dead and so are you!"

"Yes, I have died and rejoined my love. But we felt we should speak with you."

Perian waited.

"You see, my boy, it is my fault that you are here surrounded by darkness and danger, and I thought I ought to let you know that you have kept your promise to me and I am satisfied. Leave now, while you can. There is great danger here."

"And what of Alauda? Have you changed your mind about her?"

The queen stepped forward.

"What is that to you? Why are you here, young man? What do you hope for? My daughter is of royal blood and four days ago you did not know she existed. Do you presume to instruct us?"

"Your Majesty knows that best. But Angorian died trying to find the princess. Why should I do less?"

A look of contemptuous anger crossed Lastra's face.

"Don't be impertinent, boy! What do you, a beardless youth, a farm-boy from beyond Skalwood, know of such things?"

"I think I know my duty," Perian answered quietly.

"Duty! Oh, you have a duty, do you? Ambition, rather. I know you, Perian! You hope for fame and honour. You hope for wealth and power. That is what my daughter is to you! Do you deny it?"

Perian lifted his head angrily.

"That is not true! Your husband led me here and I followed. That is all."

"And you mean to stay and search? Then perhaps you are merely stupid, after all. Come, husband - I have had enough of talking to stubborn fools."

Lastra turned and dissolved into the night, but Angorian stood looking at Perian.

"I am sorry about this, my boy. But I was wrong: Alauda does not need you," and the king faded away leaving only a faint glow where he had been.

5   Lavrum

The dark of the night became deep and heavy. Perian could hardly breathe. He watched the light fading away before him. But then it started to glow brightly and a beautiful young woman appeared. She was finely dressed and her long chestnut hair fell down in cascades over her shoulders. She was smiling in a friendly way.

"I am Alauda. What do you want of me?"

Perian was speechless for a moment, then he spoke hesitantly.

"I am here to take you back to Lavrum for your coronation."

The princess frowned.

"I would rather stay here. Let the people of Lavrum find another, more fitted, to sit upon their throne. It is good here. There is peace and happiness. No jealousies, no intrigues, no cares. Perhaps you could stay here too."

"It was your father's dying wish that I should seek you and take you back."

Alauda's face changed. Now she had the look of her proud mother.

"And has he not just told you that he was wrong? Now he understands more than when he was alive. He too is happier now."

"And are you alive or dead. Your Majesty?"

The princess laughed.

"Oh, I am alive. Come here and touch me."

Perian advanced slowly and touched Alauda's out-stretched hand with his own. He shuddered. The princess and the young knight stood looking into each other's eyes.

"You are cold. Your Majesty."

"Yes. The nights are cold here."

Her voice was sucked into the night, muffled as if by a blanket. Perian stepped back and stared at the beautiful figure intently. He shuddered again and a moan came from deep within him.

"I remember a name. Your Majesty. Have you heard it? It is Kemara."

The princess cried out and, as Perian watched, her features became indistinct and she grew taller. Her hair became a dark tangle and her face aged. Her dress changed into a plain flowing black gown. Gradually the transformation was completed and Perian cowered before the vision of evil power that had replaced the beautiful princess.

"So. You know my true name. Would you now command me, farmer? You are no true knight, for all your armour and sword and Lassian steed. Come. Command me if you dare, namer of names!"

Perian straightened and looked on the face of Kemara.

"No. You know I cannot command you, any more than I can command the wind or the rising of the moon. I have come to bring Alauda away to her home. Will you release her?"

Kemara laughed but her eyes were watching Perian coldly.

"Am I supposed to admire your courage and perseverance? Shall I bow to your youth and innocence? No, all I see is impertinence and folly. You have been warned. You have been advised to go away, but you have not gone. Then you shall stay!

You wish to find Alauda?"

The sorceress placed her arms across her breast and bowed her head, then suddenly flung out her hands towards Perian.

"Go to her!"

Perian stepped forward in the dark holding his hands out before him. His foot fell on hard rock and the ringing noise of his step startled him. He took another step and his hands touched smooth wet stone. He shouted.

"Hello!"

His voice echoed strangely in the dark. No reply came. Perian turned, moved away from the rock and stretched his arms forward. He took three paces before his hands again touched cold rock. He turned to the right and shuffled carefully along keeping one hand in contact with the rock wall and the other in front of him. This time there was no obstruction and he went slowly along the narrow tunnel listening for some sound.

He stopped and shouted again.

"Hello! Is anyone there? Alauda!"

He waited, breathless, for some reply. But none came. He walked on. The tunnel was level and straight, the wall was smooth and wet and the floor was flat. Occasionally there was a stirring of the air, almost a breeze, but it was not fresh air and it came from no particular direction.

Perian walked cautiously forwards, feeling the ground with each foot before he put his weight on it. He moved, stopped, listened, then moved on again. Suddenly in mid-step his hand lost contact with the wall. He reached out but there was only air. He stepped back and found the rock with his finger tips. He had discovered a side passage or a sharp bend in the tunnel. He followed the wall round and continued walking but after a few steps he came up against an obstruction. His right hand, stretched out in front of him, touched something rough and dry. He moved closer to it and felt it with both hands, moving them up and down and across it.

"Wood. A door."

He found an iron ring in the middle of the door, grasped hold of it, and pulled. Nothing happened. He pushed. The door stood fast. He twisted the ring and pulled again. This time the door moved. He pulled again and light appeared around its edge. Finally he heaved the door open and stepped into a rock passage dimly lit by flickering oil lamps.

"Alauda! Are you there?"

A faint sound came from the far end of the tunnel: not a voice but a fluttering like wings. Perian drew his sword and hurried forward.

The passage opened into a wide, dark space, which echoed with the bird-like sound. Perian stopped at the mouth of the tunnel and listened. The noise stopped and a voice came out of the shadows.

"Who's there? Is someone there?"

"My name is Perian. I seek the Princess Alauda."

His voice echoed round the cavern. He waited for some reply.

"I am Alauda. What do you want of me?"

Perian sheathed his sword.

"Your father sent me to take you back to Lavrum."

"Lavrum? Is Lavrum real? Is there any world beyond this dark prison?"

"Lavrum is still there, waiting for the new queen. We shall go there together."

"How did you get in here? Where are you?"

"I came along a passage, through a wooden door and a lamplit corridor. I am by the entrance to the corridor."

"Stay there and I will come to you."

Alauda appeared in front of Perian, dimly lit by the light from the passage. She came towards him and as she moved her dress made a rustling, fluttering sound.

"I do not know you, Perian. You were not at the court of Lavrum."

"No. I met your father on the road to Skalbyrg and joined him in his search for you."

"My father? Where is he?"

"I am sorry to bring sad news. Your father is dead. He was murdered by men of Skalbyrg in the service of your captor, Kemara."

"Dead?"

Alauda bowed her head and tears welled from her eyes. Perian moved to her side and took her hand in his. They stood in silence for a few moments. Then Alauda raised her head and looked into Perian's eyes.

"We must try to escape. Quick, let us see if the door is still open."

They hurried down the passage to the door, but it was closed. There was neither handle nor key. Perian pushed against it, but it would not move.

"There must be another door. Do you know where, Alauda?"

"There are only four paths from the dark cavern. This is one. One leads to the lair of the dark lady, one leads to an iron gate and one leads back to the chamber where we were kept."

"Are there other prisoners, then?"

"Yes. The women of Skalbyrg are locked in a chamber on the other side of the cavern."

"We must release them. Show me the way."

Alauda took Perian's hand and led him across the dark cavern. They reached the entrance to a passage exactly like the one they had just left and Alauda led the way to the end where there was another closed door. Perian pushed and pulled at the door, but it stood firm. He shouted.

"Hello! Can you hear me in there?"

No reply came.

Perian turned away from the door and moved closer to Alauda.

"We must not submit to Kemara yet we cannot overcome her. The way out must be through the iron gate. Take me there."

Alauda took his hand again and led him to yet another passage. This one was as dark as the main chamber and they went forward slowly until they came up against the iron barrier. It was made of thick bars of iron, vertical and horizontal, making a lattice. The ends of the bars were embedded in rock and the spaces showed only darkness beyond. Perian shook the bars and exclaimed.

"This is no gate! There is no way out."

They sat down together in the dark, facing the barrier. The princess spoke softly, her voice trembling.

"There is no hope. We must submit to the will of Kemara."

Perian stretched out his hand. At the same time, Alauda reached towards him, and in the blackness of the tunnel, almost by chance, their hands met. Alauda cried out.

"Look! Light! Do you see it, Perian?"

He peered through the bars.

"There seems to be a tall mountain far away and a light shining from its top. What can it be?"

"It is growing brighter; I can see it more clearly now. It is almost like a flower."

"It is a flower. I have seen it before. And when the light of that flower can be seen there is hope. 'The shadows will lessen and burdens will be lighter, and hope will be stronger and sorrows diminished.' This must be the way!"

They stood up, watching the light beyond the bars. Keeping hold of Alauda's hand, Perian drew Sheean and tapped the iron barrier. There was a sound of fragments falling. Perian lifted the sword and attacked the bars, as if fighting an army. The noise of his blows echoed round the cavern. As he battled, Alauda at his side, the iron barrier crumbled to a heap of rusty metal. They stepped through the opening into the desert night. Perian laughed.

"Yes, I can see it. The flower of light, in the north. We must head that way, and quickly."

They took one step, then froze. A scuffling noise came out of the dark ahead of them, and the light from the north was blocked by a looming mass. Perian and Alauda went cautiously forward. There was a snorting noise and Perian spoke.

"Who's there?"

There was no reply, but then the dark shape moved and they recognised the outline of a horse's head.

"Garren!"

Perian patted the horse's flank and turned to Alauda.

"It is my horse. Now we will travel like the wind and even Kemara cannot catch us."

They mounted Garren and rode north.

The sun was setting as Garren galloped through Raiders' Gap and reached the apple tree. Here the travellers made camp for the night, falling quickly into exhausted sleep. The next morning they went down into the valley of the Siannen and on towards Skalbyrg.

When they reached the town, the morning mist was clearing and the people of Skalbyrg were beginning their day's work. At The Sentinel's Rest the travellers dismounted, entered the inn and sat down at a table. The tap-room was empty except for the inn-keeper, who was sweeping the floor. He did not notice the two newcomers until Perian spoke.

"Good morning, Belryn. May we have some breakfast?" Belryn jumped at the sound, then eyed his two customers suspiciously. He did not answer, but went, grumbling, into the kitchen. He returned bearing two plates of bread and cheese.

"You've come back, then."

He looked at Alauda, who was tired and covered in dust from the long ride.

"Who's your companion?"

"My companion is Alauda, Queen of Lavrum."

"Pardon, Your Majesty. I did not recognise you."

Alauda nodded her acceptance of the apology and spoke.

"I want two things done immediately. First, when I have eaten, bring me to the body of my royal father who was murdered here four nights ago. Then gather the men of Skalbyrg outside this inn. I would speak to them."

"Your father? King Angorian?"

"Yes," Perian interrupted, "my companion, who was killed in that cowardly attack, was Angorian the King. His death has been avenged, now due honour must be given to his remains."

"I will do as you say."

Belryn hurried away while Perian and Alauda ate their breakfast. When they had finished they went out of the inn and found the men of Skalbyrg talking in groups while they waited. Angorian's body lay on a bier, wrapped in the finest cloth that could be found in this small town.

Alauda knelt down by the bier, uncovered the face of the king, and wept. The waiting crowd gradually became silent.

Alauda stood up and addressed them.

"My Father, King Angorian, was a kind and brave man: a good father and a good king. All the people of the realm of Lavrum honour him and I will take him to Lavrum City to be buried as befits such a man.

"His murderers have been destroyed but the memory of their deed will live on. The people of Skaibyrg will be known as killers of kings. Who will sleep secure in this town, knowing of its treachery? This will be your reward for being governed by fear, for it is only fear that has led to this.

"But you need fear no longer. Perian and I have escaped from the dark lady who holds your women captive. Know these things, that the true name of the evil queen is Kemara, that her weapons are illusion and fear and that through courage and trust she may be thwarted. I say thwarted, for she may not be commanded by mere mortals. If you speak her name boldly, you will lay bare her deceits; then through courage and your united purpose you will free your women from her grasp. Go to the south; seek out Kemara and release the captives. Of old, the people of Skalbyrg were the guardians of the valley of the beautiful Siannen; now again you must be watchful."

A horse was brought for the queen. Two men took up the

bier and started towards the bridge, with Perian and Alauda following on horseback. In this way they travelled slowly along the road beside the river Siannen, towards Lavrum.

As they rode along behind the body of the old king, Perian and Alauda were subdued and thoughtful. Yet they took pleasure and comfort from each other's company, and talked quietly together of many things. They talked of their adventures, of Angorian and Lastra, of Elyn and Two Fields Farm. They grew to know each other, and, gradually, love entered their hearts.

For four days they journeyed by the gentle Siannen. On the fourth evening the little procession moved slowly across the bridge that led to the north gate of Lavrum. As they entered the city, the banner of Verumis on the palace tower was lowered and the black flag of mourning was raised. People gathered along the way to the palace, in silent homage to their dead king.

The procession climbed through the city streets to the palace, where the Council of Advice had gathered to greet the young queen. The Advisor, head of the Council, stepped forward as the bier was laid down at the palace door.

"All Lavrum mourns the death of its honoured king. My lady, if we could lessen your sorrow by any means, we would do so, but though we cannot, we do share the same bitter grief."

Alauda dismounted and replied,

"Thank you, Olendis. It is good to see you again, even when burdened with sorrow. So much has happened since I last saw the city and you, my friend, my father's friend. Now we must lay to rest the body of the king and do honour to his memory. Let all due ceremony be observed, in tribute to him and for the easing of our grief.

"But mingled with our sorrow there is some joy. For my

father's last act was to send me a rescuer to release me from great danger. This young man, Perian by name, came into darkness to save me and should be honoured and loved by all the people of our realm."

Perian got down from his horse and bowed to Olendis Alauda took his hand.

"It was no mere chance that brought Perian to the banks of the Siannen where he met my father. I believe that he has come to us for a reason. My journey was undertaken to find a man fitted to rule beside me. I have found such a man."

Perian looked startled; but before he could speak Alauda continued:

"I name Perian to be my Consort with the agreement of the Council of Advice."

So when the period of mourning was over, a wedding and a coronation were to follow.

Before the wedding Perian summoned a messenger to the throne room.

"I have a most important task for you. Listen carefully. You are to go to the northern edge of Skalwood, near where the river leaves the mountains and enters the forest. There, living on a farm known as the Two Fields, you will find my mother, Elyn. You are to speak to her these words:

'Perian your son, soon to be Consort to Queen Alauda at Lavrum, sends greetings and love. It is his wish that you should return with me to join him in Lavrum City, that your days may be lived out in comfort and peace.'

"Then you should bring her here safely and quickly, treating her with due respect and answering all her needs."

The messenger departed immediately, taking a few attendants

to ensure safe passage through Skalwood. He returned several days later with Elyn, just in time for the wedding. By then Lavrum was overflowing with visitors. People had travelled from all parts of the realm: from the farms in the west, from Skyrholm in the east and the islands beyond, from Skalwood's northern limit and from as far as Byrig in the south. Marannan, the horse-master, brought a colt for Alauda from Lassian; Craigan, Hrinan and Therior came with him. Bannig and Theyrig presented their master Tellin the iron-smith, who brought armour for the Queen. A sword, the mate to Sheean, was brought by Jurth the swordsmith. With him was his apprentice, who looked much cleaner than when Perian had last seen him. The men of Skalbyrg came, led by Belryn, who presented a hogshead of ale and told of their resolve to set out for Waslant as soon as the celebrations were finished.

Perian welcomed all who came, and retold the story of his journey to Alauda, Olendis, Elyn, and to anyone who would stop for a moment and listen. The wedding and the coronation passed in a whirl of joyous activity, and all Lavrum rang to the sounds of music and singing and laughter.

After the celebrations Elyn went to Perian.

"I will not stay here, for my home is at the Two Fields. No, I will go there and tend the tree in memory of Agravin, my uncle. Each year I will send you the fruit that has made you strong and healthy. You, in your turn, should watch over the flower on the mountain, that led you to your present place of honour. Never forget the wholesome fruit nor the light of the flower, for both are within you and have made you what you are."

So Elyn left Lavrum and the Queen and her Consort waved her farewell from the city gate

BOOK 2

Beyond the East

1 A Dragon

The days passed in peace and contentment. With the help of Alauda, Perian carried out his duties as Consort, though these were few, since the country was prosperous and peaceful. Most days were spent in happy pursuits in the palace and the city. There were balls and garden parties, plays and entertainers, but most important of all, Perian and Alauda had each other. They were as one, giving strength to each other as they performed their duties and bringing joy to each other when duty was done. Their delight in being together made all else seem unimportant: they would walk arm in arm around the palace gardens, talking and laughing for hours on end. Sometimes they would forget to eat, so great was their joy.

Each year, on Perian's birthday, the fruit was sent by Elyn and at first the King and Queen would eat some of it. But they preferred the rich and varied food from the palace kitchens, so they took to sending the fruit to the master pudding-maker to be made into a pie, covered with cream and sugar or mixed with other fruits. Though everything was tried to improve the taste, the fruit from Perian's mother was never as enjoyable as the other food from the kitchens, so as time passed they stopped eating it and instead gave it to the palace servants in a small ceremony as part of the birthday celebrations.

One year, after the giving of the fruit, Alauda noticed that Perian seemed low in spirits even though there was dancing and music all around him.

"Is something the matter, my husband? Are you unwell?"

"No, my love. I was thinking of my mother."

"Do you feel we should ask her again to come and live with us?"

"No. I was thinking of my promise to her. I should go to see the flower on the mountain."

"Yes, Perian, but why? Is there not beauty here? Why climb a mountain just to see a flower? Are not the palace gardens filled with flowers from every part of the world? What more could you desire?"

"Yes, my dear. And what beauty could any flower offer to compare with yours? You are all that I need."

He took her in his arms and she smiled up at him.

"Come, Perian! You are a man, a husband, you rule in Lavrum. You no longer have to do your mother's bidding."

Alauda laughed. Then Perian laughed too. They went to join in the dancing and the gaiety, and Perian's dark mood was forgotten.

Now life was pleasant in the valley of the Siannen. Harvests were good and ships came from the islands of the east to trade their cloth and the harvest of the sea for the timber of Skalwood, fruit from the orchards of the west valley and vegetables from the farms on the north bank. Lavrum grew in size and wealth and the farmers and traders were happy and prosperous. In Skalbyrg the women had returned and there was renewed the courage and watchfulness of former years, and no evil from the desert could enter the realm. And Perian and

Alauda were happier than all the rest for they rejoiced in each other.

Only one thing saddened the people of Lavrum: in the ten years since the wedding of their young queen she had not borne a child to inherit the throne. Perian and Alauda themselves had almost given up hope of an heir. But in the eleventh year an announcement was made throughout the land that a child was to be born to the queen. There was great joy everywhere, from the palace to the furthest part of the realm. Celebrations were held and people sang and danced to show their happiness at the news. Messages of congratulation were sent to the palace by the citizens of Lavrum and by the farmers in the west and the islanders in the east.

When the day of the birth approached there was great excitement. People came to the town from all over the country and gathered outside the walls to await the news. Perian waited too, anxious and excited. He paced restlessly up and down the corridor outside the door to his queen's chamber. The time passed slowly. From time to time Perian heard Alauda cry out in pain. Then after many hours there came a confusion of noise from the chamber. Alauda screamed, and then fell silent. Perian heard the voices of the women, hurried and anxious, and he heard a baby cry. Then there was silence. He leaned against the wall, trembling.

At last the midwife came to him, carrying a small bundle wrapped in silk and lace.

"Your Majesty, here is your child," she said, "a beautiful princess whose worth is beyond price. For your fair queen has bought this new life at the cost of her own."

"What!" said Perian. "What are you saying?"

"My lord, your wife, Queen Alauda, is dead." And the midwife broke down and wept bitterly. Her tears fell on the brow of the baby sleeping in her arms.

The king cried out and fell to the ground in a dead faint. Kind attendants carried him to his bed and he did not stir for three days. Olendis stayed at his bedside. When Perian regained consciousness he told the Advisor that he had had a nightmare and dreamed that his beloved queen had died in childbirth. Olendis told him, gently, that it was no dream, and the two of them wept.

"Let me see my daughter," said Perian, when he had recovered himself sufficiently. And the nurse brought the baby to him. He looked at the tiny child with a penetrating stare.

"You have your mother's eyes," he said to her. "You have brought great sadness to this little kingdom by your coming. I name you Magenta, but you will be called Sorrow."

He gave the child to the nurse, saying:

"I do not wish to see this child again. Attend to her needs but give her nothing that brings her joy. For she has taken all the joy from my life and I will do the same for her."

The nurse looked at the king with horror, and answered him:

"You cannot mean that, my lord. This innocent child has done harm to no-one."

Perian became angry, and shouted, "This innocent child brought death to my lovely Alauda. You will follow my orders!"

This was the first time the king had raised his voice to anyone and the servants withdrew in shocked silence; Perian fell onto his bed and wept.

The next day Perian summoned the Council of Advice to the throne room. He spoke.

"The queen is dead. Our beloved Alauda will no longer bring light to the land with her smile and her kindness. The best of wives has gone from us. But she will not be forgotten. My first act as king will be to build a beautiful tomb for her. Its beauty will remind us all of her loveliness and her joy. Send for the best stonemasons and painters and carvers of wood and we will make a memorial in the palace grounds that all the world will wonder at. And the name of Alauda will not be forgotten until the silver Siannen runs dry and all the mountains of the north are beneath the sea."

And so the queen's body was placed in a sarcophagus of gold and a tower of stone was built above it, carved and coloured by the best craftsmen in the land. All the people of the valley were put to work, quarrying stone from the mountains and carrying it to the palace, felling trees in Skalwood and floating them down the river to Lavrum.

They worked for a year, and while they worked, weeds grew in the fields, unpicked fruit rotted in the orchards and livestock became ill-fed and sick, but the tomb was not finished. Perian worked night and day, making drawings and directing the work, but as soon as some painting was finished or a carving fitted in place, he would say that it was not beautiful enough or it was not what he had in mind and so it would be removed and the work started again.

Two years went by and the farms produced scarcely enough to feed the people. The farmers complained to the Council of Advice and the traders complained, but the work carried on. The monument was nearly finished, but Perian constantly demanded small changes in the decoration. He spent all the daylight hours sitting beneath the tower gazing at Alauda's sarcophagus and in the evening he would draw up plans of the improvements he wanted.

In two years he had nearly emptied the treasury to pay for lavish ornaments for the tomb and the farms of the valley had become overgrown and desolate from neglect. Perian paid no attention to anything beyond the monument in the palace grounds.

Then one day a messenger came from Lassian, bringing a fine young horse for the king as was the custom. When he had seen the animal stabled and well cared for, he went to the king, who was seated, as usual, near Alauda's tomb. Perian was deep in thought and seemed unaware of the intruder.

"My lord?"

Perian looked up, angry at being disturbed. The messenger spoke quickly.

"I bring grave news, my lord."

"Not more delays! What is it now? Have we run out of gold leaf again? I knew we would! I told them to prepare more."

The messenger was bewildered.

"No, my lord. Not gold leaf."

"What, then?"

"I have come from Lassian. We need help. There is a dragon despoiling the land and killing our horses."

"Horses? I didn't want horses. I said yesterday that there should be a bird at each end of the sarcophagus, not horses."

"No, my lord. Our horses. The steeds of Lassian. They are being destroyed by a dragon."

"Dragon? Oh, a dragon. That explains it."

"Can you send help, Sire?"

"Yes, yes, of course. Leave me now. Farewell. And if you see a fellow mixing paints out there could you send him to me."

The messenger gave the king's order to the colourman and went to look for the Advisor. He found him in the throne room.

"Good day, my lord Olendis."

"Good day to you. And how are things in Lassian? Better than here, I hope. Are the beautiful horses well?"

"No. Not well. Indeed it is only by the greatest good fortune that I have been able to bring the young stallion, Renn, to the royal stables today. I have come for help to fight a dragon. Our lands are invaded by a black flying beast that brings fire and death."

"You have seen the king?"

"We hoped the brave strong king would take our part and defeat our enemy. But I have come from him and he cares only for Alauda's tomb."

"The queen was ever his support and his delight. Now he is less than half his former self and he embraces his grief. He no longer has the strength to fight dragons, but I will find some good men to go with you and rid Lassian of this enemy."

Twelve brave men came forward and journeyed with the messenger to destroy the flying monster. But they were themselves destroyed, for the dragon was strong and fierce and cunning. In the years that followed, men would go to the north-west hoping to prove themselves and win fame by fighting the scourge of Lassian, but none returned.

The work on the tomb continued, but only small improvements were made, as there was no more money to pay for Perian's grand designs. The country was reduced to poverty and the people of the valley struggled to grow enough to eat. And there was always the fear that the dragon would come to burn what little they had.

In the palace, Princess Sorrow was brought up as her father

instructed. None of the servants dared to go against Perian's will, though they pitied the child. Each time she showed any fondness for anything, it was taken away from her. If she became attached to playmates or servants they would be replaced. Though deprived of pleasure she still seemed to be contented most of the time. It was as if, knowing that any joy would be brief, she had learned to make as much as possible of any pleasure that came to her. She grew up to be a beautiful young woman, gentle and kind, loved and pitied by all who knew her.

So through the years, while Princess Sorrow was growing up, Lavrum was an unhappy land. Scarcely anything changed in the lives of its people, except that year by year life became a little bleaker, a little harder. The king was a remote figure, indifferent to his people's suffering. No-one had any hope that the prosperity of the old days could be restored.

Then one evening, during the twenty-seventh year of Perian's rule, a small ship sailed up the Siannen from the sea and dropped anchor below the Lavrum bridge. The watchmen on the North Gate of the town saw the beautiful craft with the golden light of the setting sun on its sail and soon the town was alive with rumour. People mounted the city walls and watched the lone sailor take in the sails and batten down the hatches, then disappear below decks as night fell. Light came from windows at the stern and no more movement was seen. Though few ships came to Lavrum in these days, nobody went to enquire of the master of the ship what his business was. But the taverns of the town were busy late into the night with people arguing whether this strange ship brought good or ill. The general view was that there had been no good news for years and so this must be a sign of some further disaster to fall.

On the following morning the watchers on the wall saw the sailor lower a small boat and row to the quayside. He jumped out, made fast, climbed the steps onto the quay and walked briskly up the road to the town. A small crowd had gathered inside the North Gate to get a closer look at the stranger and his path was blocked as he entered the town. He courteously asked the way to the palace and proceeded on his way, ignoring the questions of the bystanders.

Word of his progress was carried to the palace and the Council of Advice gathered to receive him. When he reached the throne room, he stood before the Council and looked round at each of its members.

"I would speak with the king."

The Advisor spoke for the Council.

"The king is not to be troubled. Who are you and what is your business here?"

"My name is Athellon, son of Tharlwaig, Prince of Karressinon in the south. In our land we have long known of this green valley and the town of Lavrum.

"And I have heard of your king who is not to be troubled and of the beautiful tomb. But these do not concern me. I am here to seek the hand of the sad and lovely princess, known as Sorrow, to marry her if I am fit."

There were gasps and some exclamations from the Council members. Olendis held up a hand and the room became quiet.

"Athellon of Karressinon, we thank you. We must consider this matter. Please withdraw and accept some refreshment."

The prince was conducted to an antechamber where food and drink were brought to him. Meanwhile, a page was sent to request the attendance of the princess before the Council. She came at once, and listened quietly while Olendis reported to her the words of Athellon.

"I will speak with him," she said.

This brought an immediate response from the Council. A noisy discussion broke out and carried on for some time, until Olendis called for silence and addressed the princess.

"Your Highness, I regret that we cannot allow this. It is your father's express order that your wishes be set aside. In obedience to the king's will we are unable to let you decide this matter."

"Then who is to decide? Will my father? Will you, our Councillors, make some decision?"

The Council members talked among themselves again, then one of them, Sarena by name, spoke out.

"To trouble the king would be pointless. At best we would only rouse his anger. This is a matter that we must decide for ourselves."

There was a murmur of agreement from the whole Council, but Sorrow held up her hand for silence. She spoke quietly.

"The time has come for me to have some hand in my affairs. This is not a question of a toy or playmate, it is about my future, and the future of this land. I am now a woman and heir to the throne. What is decided here is of great moment and I must have my say. And I say that I would speak with this prince from the south. What is your decision?"

Olendis answered.

"My Princess, you have spoken wisely. It shall be as you desire. Are we all agreed?"

The Council gave its consent and Prince Athellon was invited to remain in Lavrum as a guest. Sorrow and Athellon spent the days together, talking and walking in the palace grounds, telling the stories of their pasts and learning about each other. Athellon wove garlands of flowers for Sorrow's hair, wrote poems and sang songs in praise of her beauty. So the prince paid court to the princess and won her consent to their marriage.

Sorrow knew that she would have to tell the king. She consulted Olendis.

"My lord, how am I to approach my father? We have never spoken together and this is such an important matter. Would it be best if you spoke to him first?"

Olendis shook his head.

"No, Your Highness. It is time the king acknowledged you. It will not be easy, but I advise you to approach him yourself."

So she went to see her father, who was at Alauda's tomb.

As she approached he looked up and smiled.

"Alauda! How pretty you look today."

Sorrow spoke to him gently.

"No, my lord. I am not Alauda. She is dead."

He frowned with memory and pain.

"Yes. I know. Who are you, then? Why do you walk though the palace grounds, looking like my queen?"

"I am your daughter and I am called Sorrow. I have grown up in the shadow of the tomb of my mother and in the darkness of your displeasure; now is the time for a daughter to meet her father."

Perian said nothing for a moment, lost in remembering. Then he came to himself.

"What time? What brings you here against my command, to disturb me with a vision of my Alauda?"

"Custom and duty require that your permission be sought concerning my betrothal. You may neglect the duties of a king while you have loyal counsellors to serve in your stead, but you are my father and you must play your part in this matter."

"Betrothal? You are but a child. I suppose you should marry, but all in good time. Ask again when you are a little older. Now leave me."

"No. This is not to be left for another time. I have a suitor now, and he pleases me, and I him. He is a prince from the south. His name is Athellon and by him you can rid yourself of your last responsibility and devote yourself to your grief."

The king stood up and walked up and down, deep in thought.

"Very well. Send him to me and we shall see what is to be done."

The princess went quickly to find Athellon. She told him of her father's words and brought him to where Perian sat. The king did not speak at first, but looked into the prince's eyes.

"So, you wish to marry my daughter?"

"I do, with your permission."

"Are you worthy of this honour?"

"I hope so, Sire. She is content."

"I hope so too. But I would rather rely on more than hope. Proof would be better. Would you submit to a test of your worth?"

"I would."

"Good. This is the test. There is a dragon troubling my land in the north-west. Go and destroy it and you may have my daughter's hand."

Before Athellon could reply, Sorrow cried out,

"No! He will be killed, like the others. Do not ask this of us."

She seized Perian's hand, weeping.

"Father, you have taken so much from me. Must you take

Athellon too?"

But the prince came to her and took her gently in his arms.

"I am not afraid, Sorrow, I would do more than this for you. And think what the death of the dragon will mean to your people. The king has the right to lay this duty on me."

He turned to Perian.

"Very well. I will undertake this. You and your dragon will find that I am not easily defeated. I have heard how you overcame the dark hag of the desert to release your love. I will do no less for mine."

Perian stood and looked at the prince sadly.

"I do not wish you ill. There was a time when I would have faced the monster myself. If you succeed, you will bring back some joy to this realm. Take my armour and my good sword Sheean and Renn, my Lassian horse. They will serve you well. Good fortune attend you!"

So Athellon, well armed, rode out of Lavrum and into Skalwood, carrying the hopes of all the people with him.

At this time Skalwood was dark and dangerous. Wild animals and bandits attacked any traveller who tried to pass through. Most people took a longer journey rather than risk their lives, but Athellon was in a hurry. Though he had to defend himself twice against men and twice against wolves, he passed through in safety and emerged from the forest in two days.

He found himself at the foot of the mountains he had seen from Lavrum and started riding westwards. Before long he came to a farm and stopped to ask the way to Lassian. An old woman came out of the small log house to greet him. She peered at him curiously.

"Are those the arms of the King of Lavrum? Is that you,

Perian?"

"No, old lady, I am not the king, though I bear his arms. My name is Athellon and I am sent by him to Lassian to fight the dragon."

"Well, never mind. You look tired. Get down off that big horse and I will give you some refreshment."

Elyn fetched him wine and fruit.

"How is my son?"

"Your son?"

"Perian. The king. When I last saw him he was but a boy, newly crowned. How long ago? But I send him fruit every year, just as I promised. How is he? Do tell me."

"He is much borne down since the death of his queen. I cannot say he is well."

"That's strange. When you see him, ask him if he eats the fruit. And ask him about the flower. Will you do that for me?"

Athellon agreed to carry the message and continued on his way, taking some fruit with him. Following Elyn's directions he found the Siannen where it turned north and followed it to Lassian. As he approached the town he could see the devastation caused to all the land around. There were burnt and blackened trees, grass turned to ash and the carcasses and skeletons of horses scattered about.

When he reached the town it was quiet and the wooden gates were closed.

"Hallo there, Lassian! Open your gates for an emissary from Lavrum."

A head appeared above the parapet over the gate, and Athellon was scrutinised carefully.

"From Lavrum, eh? What's your business?"

"Killing dragons."

"Oh. It's a while since we had one of them. You'd better come in."

The gates opened and Athellon entered the town. Lassian was a town for horses. All the streets were broad and all the people were on horseback, even small children. A crowd of riders gathered round Athellon as he rode through the gates and at first they ignored him and examined his mount.

"That's a king's horse," one said. "Are you the king?"

"No. My name is Athellon and I have been sent by King Perian to rid you of the dragon. Where can I find it?"

"Oh, don't worry about that. You ride up into the hills and it'll find you."

Some of the people laughed sourly. Athellon wheeled his horse round and rode back out of the gate and towards the hills.

Soon he saw the signs of the dragon's activities. The few trees that remained were burnt black, some of them still smoking. The further he went, the fewer were the living trees, until he was travelling through a wasteland of charcoal and scorched earth. The smell of burning was stronger and smoke made his eyes smart. Eventually Renn refused to go any further, so Athellon tethered the frightened beast and proceeded on foot. Although the stench of rotting flesh was all around him, he could see neither the dragon nor its lair.

But the dragon saw him. It glided silently on outstretched wings high above the prince, watching his progress through the blackened land. It swooped down low over his head, casting a dreadful shadow, and landed in his path. Its vast form towered over him, its hard scales gleaming blackly. Athellon froze before the gigantic beast and put his hand to his sword. He watched the dragon warily, avoiding its blood-red eyes. But the monster made no move to attack. Instead it spoke, in a deep hissing voice.

"So, a visitor to my humble abode. You come armed and armoured, little man. Surely you are not here to hurt me? I have done you no harm."

"My apologies, mighty dragon, but I have travelled some distance for the sole purpose of destroying you. It is hardly likely that I will depart before making the attempt."

"Yes, little dragon-slayer. There you are right. It is hardly likely that you will depart."

The dragon made a coughing sound that might have been laughter. Athellon drew Sheean and held it aloft.

"We shall see which of us will leave this place! Let us test the temper of my sword in your flesh."

"No! Look about you, brave knight. See the scattered bones of dragon-slayers. They foolishly tried their weapons against me and now they are greatly honoured in Lavrum but they are no less dead. You cannot imagine how tedious it is, crushing the small bodies of men who place themselves within my grasp. It is more fun chasing the horses hereabouts, and there's more meat on them. No, let us play a different game."

"What do you propose?"

"A battle, not of swords and claws, but of wits. Who knows a dragon's name may destroy it. Guess my name and you may strike me with your little sword. Fail and you will lay down the sword and run from me. You will not escape, but I will enjoy the chase. I do enjoy a chase."

The dragon laughed again. Athellon thought for a moment then sheathed his sword.

"Very well. Do I get a clue?"

"Oh yes. A clue. Here is a riddle to tell you my name. Guess it if you can."

And the dragon recited:

"Kings, ever masters, always rule above;
Ever below, they are slaves to their love.
Masters of men, but servants of their grief,
Always they come begging for relief.
Rule is for the loveless, soarer on wings;
Above flies the dragon, ruler of kings."

Athellon laughed.

"But you are wrong, great dragon. I stand here in the name of love and I will defeat you."

The dragon lifted its head and gave forth a roar that echoed around the hills, and flames came from its nostrils. It lowered its head until the massive jaw nearly touched the ground.

"Guess my name! If you can. Let us see whether your love has aided your wits or dulled them."

Athellon stood thinking. The dragon towered over him, snorting impatiently.

"Come on. Come on. If you haven't guessed it by now, you never will."

"But I have, clever dragon! I have found it woven into the words of your riddle. Your name is Kemara and I have won the right to strike at you unhindered."

The dragon started to speak, but before it could make a sound Athellon leapt forward, drawing his sword. He dived under the dragon's chin and thrust Sheean upwards into its throat. Hot black blood poured from the wound, covering Athellon completely. He leapt back out of reach of the dragon's claws and watched the death throes. The dragon roared in anger and fear. It thrashed and fought against its fate. Gradually the great beast settled to the ground as the strength went from its legs. At last it lay still and a final fiery breath came from its nostrils, making a smoky mist. As Athellon watched, the smoke formed into a dense black cloud and took on the form of a tall woman in black. She looked on Athellon with contempt.

"You have destroyed my outer form, but you cannot destroy me! I am Kemara, eternal and unconquerable. We will meet again."

She dissolved once more into smoke and was carried away on the wind.

Athellon returned to his horse and rode to Lassian. When he told the people of the death of the dragon, there was joyous celebration and a great feast was held in honour of Athellon. The feast lasted three days and many songs were sung in praise of the young prince. From that time the name of Athellon was honoured above all others in Lassian.

After the celebrations the dragon's head was hewn from its body by the men of Lassian and brought to the river, where it was placed on a raft. The people of Lassian brought treasures for Athellon and piled them beside the monstrous head until the raft was nearly swamped. So Athellon and Renn drifted away down the river with many of the townspeople following along the bank, waving and cheering until the current carried the raft out of their sight.

As he floated along the Siannen, the news of Athellon's triumph spread, and people came to the river to see the dragon's head and cheer the hero. By the time he reached Lavrum the people of the town were waiting on the bridge and both banks.

The whole of the Council of Advice was on the quay with the king and Princess Sorrow. A great cheer went up as the raft came to rest by the quay. Then there was complete silence while Athellon spoke.

"Your Majesty, I bring you a gift."

Another cheer from the crowd.

"I bring it for you, for your people, and as a token of my love for the Princess Sorrow."

The crowd roared its approval, and then Perian answered.

"No words of mine could be more eloquent than the acclaim of my people. You have brought relief to a troubled land and a new light into the darkness of my heart. Take the hand of my daughter and dwell with us in our beautiful valley. Since her birth she has been known as 'Sorrow', but her true name is Magenta. Now let Magenta, whose coming brought sorrow, and Athellon, who has brought new hope, be joined together forthwith."

Again wild cheering broke out.

Magenta smiled at Athellon, who climbed up from the raft, took her hand and stood beside her. This brought even louder shouts from the people. The royal party stood for a while, acknowledging the crowd's joyful noise. Then the king, the prince and princess, and the Council of Advice, returned to the town, followed by the boisterous throng. A groom from the royal stables led Renn back to the palace behind them, and even he was cheered and praised by the delighted people.

The next day, when the travellers were rested and Athellon had spoken to Perian and Magenta of the dragon, the town of Lassian, and his journey, he said:

"My love, I think I must tell some parts of this tale to your father alone. Will you forgive me?"

Magenta smiled. She kissed them both, and left the room, saying to Athellon, "As long as you promise to meet me in the garden as soon as you have finished. I will wait by the fountain."

Athellon looked after her, smiling, until Perian coughed gently.

"My lord, forgive me."

"No matter, dear boy - I do understand, you know."

"Yes. But there are things I must tell you that I do not fully understand, and that seem to me to be of great importance."

"Go on."

"Well, firstly I remember that after the dragon's death I seemed to see a vision, a woman evil yet fair, who spoke scathingly to me and named herself Kemara."

Perian started to his feet.

"She told me that her spirit had dwelt in the dragon's body, and that she was undying and would return."

"Yes. Indeed she will. I know of Kemara, and will tell you in due course all you need to know of her. But what else have you to tell?"

"On my journey north I came to a small farm on the edge of Skalwood, and there met an old lady who was kind to me, and told me that she was Elyn, your mother."

"My mother?"

Perian sat down again, slowly. A shadow of memory passed across his face.

"She gave me a message. She asked whether you still eat the fruit, and about the flower."

Perian sat up and stared, as if seeing something far away. He sat quite still, his body tense as if listening to distant voices. Then he closed his eyes and tears forced their way out and down his cheeks. He hid his face in his hands and started to sob. Soon he was howling like a child. Athellon leaned forward and touched the king's shoulder, but Perian turned away. The prince waited, and eventually the sobbing ceased. Perian spoke again.

"When I became Alauda's consort I forgot that there was more to do. I thought it was the end of a story, and so it was. But it was the beginning of another. I took my strength from Alauda, and when she left me I fell into despair. I am not now fit to be king. I must eat the fruit again, and go to see the flower."

Athellon said, "My lord, I understand little of what you are saying, but I cannot believe that you need think so ill of yourself. Let us think now of the better times to come in Lavrum, and not of the sorrows of the past."

"You are very kind," Perian answered, "but some of my griefs are very deep. Leave me now and go to Magenta, and make plans for your wedding day. I will rejoice with you then, but I must be alone for a while now."

The wedding of Athellon and Magenta took place a few days later. It was a glorious day of smiles and happiness. People came from all over the valley to swell the numbers of the joyful crowd. After the ceremony, conducted by Olendis in the grand ballroom of the palace, the celebrations continued into the following day. The town was taken over by music, laughter and noise. Dancing people filled the streets with life and gaiety.

Once the celebrations were over Athellon and Magenta set to work. Using the treasures that had come from Lassian they travelled about the valley helping the hard-pressed farmers to make good the losses of past years. Ploughs were repaired, fences were mended, and food was bought for the needy. Once again, ships came up the river to Lavrum and old trade-routes were re-opened.

Perian lived quietly, taking little part in the work. Sometimes he would make a suggestion but usually it was about something which had already been done by the prince and princess. It was they who reminded him when his birthday was approaching.

"Is it really? Yes, I believe you are right. My mother will send the fruit. That is good. I will eat some fruit and that will strengthen me to climb the mountain to the flower."

But when his birthday came no fruit arrived. Another fine horse came from Lassian; Mela, a grandson of Garren who had carried Perian into the desert long ago. But there was no word from Elyn. Perian sent a messenger to her to fetch some fruit and make sure she was well.

When the messenger returned, he went to the king.

"I bring sad news, my lord. Your mother has died and is buried beside the great tree you told me of. There was no fruit on the tree."

Perian looked at the man sadly.

"Then there is no hope for me."

2 Leaving

One morning, a few months after his birthday, Perian woke up and realised that there was a chill in the air. He shivered, and snuggled more closely under his blankets. But he could not get back to sleep, so instead sat up resolutely, and flinched at the sharp stiffness in his shoulders. He looked around the familiar room. The walls were the same as usual, mellow golden stone just beginning to draw some richness from the waxing light of morning. The same trees were visible through the window. As Perian watched, a leaf detached itself and floated slowly down beyond his sight. He shivered again, pulled back his covers and lowered his feet to the floor. His knees hurt. His feet were cold. He noticed the thinness and pallor of his legs.

"I am old," he said aloud. "I am old."

He dressed, not calling his servants but hastily getting into whatever clothes came to hand, slipped cautiously through the still-quiet passages of the palace, saddled his own horse and rode out past the astonished, drowsy sentry towards the North Gate of the city. Here too the watchman was startled to see his king, but Perian gave him only a brief nod before heading away north as fast as Mela's morning eagerness could carry him.

Before the sun was well risen, before the air was truly warm, he was approaching the outskirts of the forest. He slowed down and began to look about him. It was becoming yet another of the smiling days they had come to expect that summer. There was peace in everything, in the heraldic blue of the sky, the soft lush green of the grassland, the deeper green of Skalwood ahead of him. Yet as Perian watched, the trees were tossed by a freak gust of wind sweeping in from the sea away to the east, and as they tossed they shed each a small flurry of yellow-gold leaves. He looked up at the strengthening sun, sighed, and rode, more slowly now, towards the forest.

Under the trees all was still, with hardly a sign of life. Perian followed a broad ride he had often travelled before, but after a while turned aside into the wildness of the trees. He crossed a stream. He sat for a while on a grey rock while his horse cropped the grass and a squirrel watched him covertly. He mounted again and rode ever deeper into the forest, where there were trees of great age and immense size, that blotted out more and more of the light and the sky.

Gradually Perian began to be aware of something between the trees away to his right. It was whiteness, or some light-source, and he saw it with the corner of his eye for several minutes before curiosity compelled him to turn his head and look straight at it. Finding that he still could not make out what it was, he turned his horse towards it.

The trees here were enormous, of great girth, many hollow and rotting below but still leafy far above. The ground underfoot was knotty with roots and made bad going, so that when he was drawing near the brightness between the trees, Perian was forced to dismount and lead his horse slowly, picking a way. This kept his attention focused on the ground, and he was startled when Mela suddenly stiffened his legs and neck and refused to take another step forward. Perian concentrated for some minutes on trying to coax the beast, forgetting entirely about the thing he was trying to examine. It was only exasperation with Mela's stubbornness that made him finally turn around and look at what the creature was worriedly regarding over his master's shoulder. And then he too was still.

Between and around the trees there swirled a thickness of grey-white mist or vapour, impenetrable to sight as a heavy velvet curtain. Perian stretched out a hand and tried to touch it, but the tendrils pulled away from him and left him grasping.

"What is this wonder?" he said. "Is anyone here? Show yourself!"

There was no reply, only a low, unhappy noise from Mela. Perian turned to him, soothed him, then led him a little way back into the trees before tethering him securely to a branch. That done, he came back to the edge of the mist and stood looking into it. After a few moments he stepped forward; but he had only taken one or two steps when the mist, solidifying as it moved, poured itself towards him and pressed against him, preventing his further advance. Perian halted, and watched in astonishment as the motion and fluidity of a moment before hardened into a flat, gleaming surface like glass or ice; and as the word 'mirror' came into his head, the rippling ceased and he saw himself reflected in a broad and crystal-clear expanse of adamantine hardness. His fingers made no impression on it at all. His face looked back at him, and he saw to his annoyance that he looked awe-struck and overwhelmed. He drew himself up and spoke again.

"Whose is this enchantment? Speak! Reveal yourself and your purpose!"

As if triggered by his voice, the surface of the mirror rippled again, and Perian cried out wordlessly as it showed him a scene he had not beheld with his own eyes for more than twenty years. There was the mountain, and the tree, and his mother's house; and running towards the house a small boy, perhaps seven or eight years old; and Perian saw that it was himself. Tears filled his eyes as he saw in the mirror his mother standing outside the old house, bending to embrace him.

"Mother!" But she could not hear him, and as he struggled with his tears, the picture dissolved and changed.

Now Perian saw the night-dark tangle of a thorn bush on the mountain-side, and himself, aged fourteen, kneeling rapt before it, gazing into its darkness at the flower that shone there. He leaned against a tree, trembling.

The picture, shimmering, changed to show him an icy mountain waste, through which his younger self staggered in an agony of effort, and he saw again where the crystal spring leapt joyous in the wasteland and felt the ecstasy of that triumph. He watched his own return to the place of the flower, where the wizard waited to greet him.

Faster and faster the images rolled by him, darkness in the desert and his wife's face laughing on their wedding day; the return of Prince Athellon with the dragon's head. Perian cried out, "Stop, oh please, stop, leave me alone!" Obediently the mirror clouded over, dissolving back into a tumbling mist among the trees, before vanishing completely from Perian's sight. Mela let out a glad snort of relief; and Perian, looking up, found himself kneeling at the feet of the wizard.

The arms that raised and embraced him were still strong, the shoulders still broad, and the wizard's hair showed only a slight sprinkling of grey; Perian's was white as snow. The king leaned heavily against his friend and wept. When he grew calmer, the wizard encouraged him to sit down on a fallen tree, and sat beside him.

"Perian, my friend. It is good to see you again."

"I am glad to see you; that is, as far as I can be glad on this hideous day of fears and enchantments. Did you make that magic mirror? Did you mean to torment me? Who could be so cruel to me?"

"Not I. This is an ancient magic of these woods, neutral in itself but woken by whatever mood is in the one who seeks to enter the mist. You have brought forth the images of your own regret, Perian. I came to you, across many hundreds of miles, because I heard you cry out in your despair and sought to help you."

Perian gripped his friend's hand. "Then I thank you for your care of me. But what help is there for old age, loss, failure? For the running-out of time and the fear of death? All come to this moment, I suppose, and cry out against the time they have wasted, the journeys they have not taken, the love they have not given. But it is too late. Too late for me, is it not?"

The wizard smiled.

"It is never too late, they say. What would you do if you were free, Perian?"

"But I am not free. There is the kingdom to think of."

"Perian, you may set yourself free, by the custom of Lavrum. Abdicate, and let Magenta be queen. Athellon will be at her side."

Perian looked at him in silence. Then he said:

"I never thought of that."

"Well then; where would you journey, and what would you seek?"

"Perhaps I should climb the mountain again and look upon the flower."

"That was a vision of your youth, Perian. You are too old to climb that mountain now."

Perian reflected. "Then I will go east." he said. "I shall journey to the sea, before it is too late, and look upon its wonders, and find out its secrets. Maybe I shall come to the springs of the morning, where light is born."

The wizard smiled again.

"Maybe you will," he said.

Perian rode back into Lavrum in the grey dusk. Magenta and Athellon were relieved at his return, but when he told them of his plan to travel to the east they grew concerned again.

"But why?" asked Magenta. "What do you want to find, or see, or bring back? What would be the point of it? Father, a man of your age cannot simply wander off into the blue for no particular reason. You are needed here. I had thought you were safe and happy here. Why should you go and risk all sorts of dangers and leave those who love you to worry about you?"

"Indeed, sir," added the prince, "your people would sorely miss you. They love their king. Surely the time for adventure is the time of youth; and had you not many wondrous adventures as a young man?"

"Oh," cried Perian, "how can I make you understand? One lifetime is not enough to see a thousandth of the wonders that there are in the world. I am caged here, growing older, and there is so much I have never seen and do not know. You are more than able to rule. This is my last chance to find what I seek."

"What do you seek. Father?" asked Magenta, softly.

"I cannot say. Only that it burned at the heart of the flower and flowed in the stream and rode with me into the desert; and

I have lost it or neglected it and time is running out. I want to find that again, before I die."

And they saw that Perian was determined to go. So they agreed to his abdication and the prescribed ceremony was carried out within a few days. Magenta was now Queen of Lavrum.

So Perian set out on a bright autumn morning, and the people gathered in the narrow streets to watch him depart. Mela stepped out steadily, undisturbed by the shouts that rose here and there.

"Good luck, Your Majesty!" some cried.

"Peace attend your path, King Perian." some called out as he passed.

Others were reluctant to see him go.

"Stay, my lord, do not leave us!'

"When will you return?"

"Come home soon, Your Majesty!"

Within the shadow of the North Gate, Perian reined Mela and turned to speak to the crowd.

"My people, do not think that I leave you easily or gladly. Your kindness to me touches my heart; I fear I have little deserved it."

A roar of disagreement from the crowd.

"However that may be, I must go. I cannot hope to explain why - even my daughter does not truly understand, you know."

They laughed, and cheered again.

"But remember that to each of us there may come one day some overwhelming desire, to seek adventure it may be, or to travel into strange and distant lands, and the desire may be too strong for us to resist. My people, my love for you is deep and if I come not again to our city -." At this the protesting cries of the people swelled too loudly for him to continue. Mela performed a nervous, sideways skittering movement, and by the time Perian had him under control the crowd was quiet again.

"If I come not again to Lavrum, the memory of your devotion will stay with me always. Farewell and bless you, my dear people. Peace be on the city and realm of Lavrum."

And the people cried as with one voice, "Peace attend your path. King Perian!"

Perian rode out towards the sunrise with these countless good wishes sounding in his ears. He did not look back.

Two days' journey brought him to the high ground above Skyrholm, and here he dismissed his two servants and their pack-animals.

"But, Your Majesty, we have promised the queen that we will care for you faithfully!"

"And so you have, Sellan, and the last of your faithful deeds will be to obey my order that you leave me."

"Oh, my lord, we dare not."

"Oh, Sellan, you dare not stay, for then my royal displeasure will fall upon you heavily. Come, man, I am not a child. It is freedom I desire, freedom such as I have not known since I was a boy in Skalwood. Go back to the queen and tell her that I will do very well by myself, and bear to her and to Athellon her Consort my affectionate greeting. Only be off, and quickly!"

And he spurred Mela at them in mock anger, so that they hastened away towards Lavrum, with many a glance behind. Perian watched them out of sight, then dismounted.

Opening his saddle-pack, he brought out the plain, well-used garments he had kept for the purpose, and shed his royal attire. The body-armour he concealed, along with his shield, in a dense thicket of gorse where it seemed unlikely to be found by any wayfarer. The bags of gold coins Magenta had thrust upon him proved a nuisance, but he concealed them about his person and in the bundles he was to carry with him. Sheean he wrapped in an old rag and laid it by while he attended to Mela.

"Sorry, old fellow," he murmured, stripping the magnificent beast of his fine leather saddle and bridle, coating his legs and flanks with mud, tangling his silken mane, and tossing only a blanket over his back and a rope halter over his noble head. Lashing a bag of food and spare clothes, together with the bundle containing the sword, across Mela's back with a length of rope that also served to secure the blanket, Perian remounted.

A few hours later, Perian rode down the one winding street of Skyrholm and turned in at the Barrel House Inn. He bought ale, cheese, and coarse bread, and sat down in a corner. Many of those drinking gave Perian a courteous "Good evening" or at least a nod. The servant-girl told him he could get a bed for the night and stabling for his horse. Perian bought more ale, and found himself drawn into a circle of drinkers.

"South, that's the way to travel!" one man was asserting loudly. "South where it's warm day and night, and the wine is cheap and the women willing and the pickings easy for an honest merchant."

There was a roar of laughter at the fellow's claim to be honest, but Perian said eagerly,

"Tell me of the south! I have never been there."

The merchant eyed him, winked at his fellows, and said:

"Well, you see, it's a different world down there. Everyone rich as kings, gold and jewels used as coin in the market-place, fruits rare and delicious falling from every tree, dark-eyed women that don't answer a man back, and wine such as you'd never believe after this thin northern ale."

He drained his cup, and everyone looked expectantly at Perian. The king hastily ordered more ale for them all, and said, "Go on! Go on, it sounds wonderful."

The merchant went on for some time. By the time he had finished all the truth and most of the lies, he and Perian were leaning affectionately against each other and gesticulating expansively with their ale-mugs.

"Really?"

"Honestly, my friend, as sure as I sit here, rubies large as eggs and gold in heaps!"

"And it's always warm?"

"And the wine is plentiful."

"There's fruit on every tree?"

"As much as you can eat."

"Are the women really beautiful?"

"Yes, young and beautiful, every one."

"And kind and warm and friendly?"

Perian began to cry, but his new friend did not notice, since at this point he fell asleep with his head on the table in a pool of spilt ale. The kindly serving-girl, seeing Perian's distress, led him gently up the stairs and left him snoring loudly on his bed.

In the bright morning light he woke feeling both nauseous and aching in the head. The first condition eased as soon as he moved, because he was violently sick. He groaned. He groaned louder. But the servant was occupied in clearing up after the breakfasts of the other travellers, all long since up and away, and not for two hours did her duties bring her clambering up the attic stairs, by which time the stench in Perian's room was distinctly unpleasant.

"Well!" She stood in the doorway, clutching his bundle and saddle-pack that he had left carelessly in the stables the previous night, and looked at him, her nose wrinkled and her eyes laughing.

"Thought you wasn't used to it. Stole away from some great house, haven't you? And stolen your master's sword, you wretch. We like honest guests here, not rogues. No doubt it's fine wine you're used to, not our good rich ale."

Perian groaned again, and she switched from her light mocking to a gentle concern. Tenderly she cleaned both Perian and the room, gave him clean water to drink and a little soft white bread to nibble, and told him he would find her below when he felt strong enough. To his surprise, he soon did, and went down to find her tossing his sheets and covers over a rope strung between the back door of the inn and a tree in the yard. He watched for a moment. Suddenly she said:

"Lend a hand, then! Didn't your mother ever teach you better manners than that?"

"Yes. Yes, she did, of course," said Perian. He took the washing from her and spread it neatly out to catch the brisk autumn wind, then went to the stable to see that Mela was well looked after. He was, and was pleased to see his master. The girl had left the yard when Perian returned, and he sought her in the kitchen.

"You have been so good to me. What is your name?"

"Anna. And you?"

"Perian," he said without thinking. But she only laughed, and said it was a fine thing to be named after the king.

"And what happened to you?" she asked. "Did you get too old to fight, and your lord threw you out?"

"Yes, that's it. And the sword is my own."

"Oh, dear, I never meant that - I can see you're no thief. Used to finer things than this, I daresay," and she gestured around the kitchen.

"Yes - but I should like to help you, you have been good to me."

And so the king spent the day cleaning, polishing, peeling vegetables and preparing fish stew for the evening trade. His own bowl of the stew went down well at supper-time, tasting better than he could remember palace food tasting of late. And afterwards he consumed a moderate amount of the good brown ale, chatting amicably with some of the local fishermen and farmers. He stayed up to help Anna with the scouring and rinsing of plates and mugs, and was glad enough to follow her up the attic stairs around midnight.

"Goodnight, Anna."

"Goodnight, Perian. Sleep well, tonight!" and she laughed at him, gently.

Over breakfast he told her that it was time for him to move on, then went to get his things ready and Mela equipped. He led the horse out into the yard and hitched him near the kitchen door. Anna was sitting at the kitchen table in tears.

"Anna."

"Yes, Yes, Perian," and she jumped up and tried to cover her weeping. He came in.

"Don't cry, dear child. I must get on, time is short at my age, you know."

"What is so important that you must dash away just as we were getting comfortable together? It's a lonely life, Perian, and you've been kind and helpful - I'm not used to that. Can't you spare me a day or so?'

He shook his head.

"I want to see the bright Southland, Anna, and feel the sun warm my old bones. I'll come back, maybe, with a fine gift for you - how would that please you?"

"I'd rather come with you." She turned away as she spoke.

"Thank you," he said softly. "If only you could. But my journey may take me on dangerous paths. I would not want any harm to befall you."

Perian kissed her fleetingly on the brow and hastened out to unhitch, mount, and turn Mela all in one rapid movement. She rushed after, to watch the slight, bowed figure on the great black horse as it dwindled away towards the river.

Perian rode quickly down to the estuary, where the Siannen widened to a sluggish width of brown water. It was approaching high tide, and he hailed the flat-bottomed ferry from the far shore. It was quiet here, for across the water was a wild land, a rough road through the hills and along the coast, with only a bit of grazing fit for sheep here and there, or marshes where some hardy souls might go wildfowling. Birds were all about him, swan and oyster-catcher and mallard and the bright shelduck, moving upstream as the mudflats were slowly covered by the encroaching sea. The ferryman greeted him, as he led Mela aboard.

"Going far?"

"As far south as I can get," Perian asserted.

"Huh! Do better heading west and down the Great South

Road, if you ask me."

"Why so?"

"Trouble with robbers these many years. We petitioned the King's Grace for a knight or two to clear this way - folks down the coast where 'tis good farmland likes to trade a bit here in Skyrholm as well as Lavrum. Only nought's done yet, that's kings for you," and he spat noisily into the water.

"The king has had his troubles, but perhaps the Prince Athellon, the dragon-slayer, will take this in hand now."

The ferryman snorted.

"And the Siannen may flow up to the mountains."

Perian gazed for a moment up the river towards Lavrum, but then fixed his attention on the southern shore, as the ferry neared its landing.

The coast road was an ancient trackway that wound up and down, always close to the shore because of the hills inland, but sometimes high above the sea and looking down onto a rocky shore lashed with white waves, and sometimes level beside a narrow strip of shingle beach. Perian urged Mela on towards the more pleasant, fertile coastal plain to the south-west. Here there were farms and hamlets and the coast road joined the Great South Road at the village of Byrig. Once, halting at the top of a cliff, Perian looked far out to sea and glimpsed the islands to the north-east, dark masses in the blue expanse of water.

"I will go there one day," he said to Mela. "There's time for a visit to the south first."

The horse shook his mane and plodded on down the road. After a few minutes Perian urged him to a trot again.

About midday he was passing a stretch of the shingle beach, when a ragged boy appeared, starting up from the roadside towards the sea and crying out, "Alms! My lord, my noble master, alms! Spare a copper for a poor wretch, Sir!"

And the king stopped. He even dismounted. But before he could speak to the skinny waif in front of him, a voice addressed him from behind.

"We are three, and all armed," it said, "so I advise you just to step away from that there fine animal you no doubt swiped up the coast, and let us be having him. No need for anyone to get hurt, not on a nice sunny day like this, eh?"

Perian turned, and saw three scruffy louts with rusty but sharp swords pointed at him. At his side the boy sniffled, "Oh, I'm sorry, I'm sorry," so that the largest of the men yelled at him.

"Give over, Ilo, you snivelling rat!" he said, and kicked him so hard that he tumbled over the low bank of marram-grass down onto the shingle. Perian gave a great shout, reached into his bundle swiftly, and swept the bright blade of Sheean through the air before the robbers. At first they fell back, but rallied and despite Perian's greater skill were on the point of overcoming him.

Behind Perian stood Mela the war-horse, proud and steady amid the noise of fighting, and he did not move from his master's side. They both stood firm until one of the robbers, aiming a clumsy, fierce blow at Perian from one side, sliced his dirty blade across Mela's neck, and at once the horse's life-blood was spurting from the dreadful wound. Within seconds he was on his knees, and the robbers with one accord turned and ran. None of them dared to face the anger that shone now in Perian's eyes. Perian paid no heed to them as he knelt to support the dying stallion's head. There was only a flicker of life in the soft eyes now, but Perian through his tears talked to

Mela lovingly, caressing and kissing the velvet nose. And at the darkening of Mela's eyes Perian fell forward and lay across the great body sobbing, until he felt hands tugging at him.

"Sir, Sir, please, oh I'm sorry, Sir, the beautiful horse, I'm sorry, but we must go, they might come back, don't let them find me, oh Sir, they'll kill us too, please come!"

Perian got up slowly, still weeping, and allowed himself to be led back north along the old road, towards the estuary. Sheean he picked up as he came to where it lay in his path. Several hours of trudging brought them to the bank of the river, where the water was low and the sandpipers scuttled peeping across the mudflats. Sitting down heavily on a tuft of reedy grass, Perian looked for the first time directly at his companion; he saw a pale, dirty face, thin and anxious in the thickening light of dusk.

"Poor boy!" he said. "What is your name?"

"Ilo," the child almost whispered. "I'm sorry - oh, so sorry! Your lovely horse; and the blood - so much blood -" and he burst into hysterical sobs. Perian gathered the boy close and soothed him, rocking him in his arms until the weeping died away.

"Are you not cross with me?" The voice was small and tremulous.

"No. I am very upset, in pain - but I can see you did not mean to do anything wicked. I must take the blame for my horse's death. It was I who chose to take the coast road south. The ferryman warned me I might meet with robbers. How came you with those men, Ilo?"

"They came to our house - down the coast, south, we fished for our living, and they killed father, and hurt mother so much she died too, and kept me to train for fooling travellers, they said any fool would stop for a child and then they could rob them. I never wanted to, only they beat me, you see."

"Yes." said Perian. "I see all too clearly, my child. Will you stay with me now? I will try to be kind to you, if you will be a friend to me."

"Me? Fat lot of good I'd be, Sir."

"Well, now. Fishing, you said. So you can handle boats, no doubt? How old are you, Ilo?"

"Twelve, Sir. And I've been in boats all my life. I could swim before I could walk, Sir."

Perian gazed out over the sea for a while before asking, "Could you handle a sailing boat? Big enough to sail to the east, with me to crew for you?"

"Yes, I could do that. But where would we go?"

"I should like to journey to the Islands."

3 The Tower

That night they huddled in a dug-out shelter in the side of a sand-dune, sung to sleep by the wind in the marram. By high water next morning they were at the Barrel House consuming huge breakfasts, watched by Anna and such loiterers as had time to spend drinking in the morning.

"But you could both have been killed! And that poor, dear animal, such a beauty! Whatever possessed you to go that way, Perian? You must have been mad."

"No, not mad, but certainly misled. Now there's the future to think of. You hurry this boy into a bath, while I go and get him some decent clothing. Then we could both do with a bit more rest, in a bed this time, and some of your stew this evening, and tomorrow we'll have some buying to do - won't we, Ilo?"

The boy nodded eagerly. Anna sighed heavily and shooed Ilo out towards the kitchen and the large copper tub. Perian finished his drink, listening to the splashes and laughter; then went off on his errand.

The next day was a busy one; Perian and Ilo were down among the wharves soon after breakfast, prospecting for a likely craft, and settling at last for an old but still seaworthy sailing-boat called Islander.

"That's a good name, Ilo. What do you think of her?"

"She's strong-looking, my lord, not fancy but she'll get us there."

"I'll take your word for it, Ilo. Do you think we can handle her?'"

"Oh yes, Sir, if you follow my lead."

The boat's former owner watched with interest while Ilo kept Perian beating about within hailing distance of Skyrholm until the tide started running out too fast to continue. A stiff and weary crewman staggered back to the inn with his still energetic young skipper, to swallow a welcome draught of ale and to dry out before the huge fire in the parlour.

"I don't know!" scolded Anna. "One crazy idea after another!"

"It's all right, Anna. I shall take care this time, you'll see. No foolish venture this, but the journey I set out to make when I left my home."

"Hmm! A fine pair you are to be setting sail in the autumn. You won't convince me there's any sense in it."

She protested when they set out again, but there was still daylight left to trade by, and Ilo and Perian now acquired plenty of hard rations, weatherproof clothes, and changes of warm undergarments, against their departure – which was planned for the next day. All that remained was to fill the cask in the boat with fresh water, stow their new goods in the lockers with Sheean (wrapped in oilskin) and set sail to the east and the first island.

The next noon found Perian tossing on the cold wet sea, trying to learn all that Ilo wanted him to learn about the management of boats. The journey north-east towards Sewil, the first island, was relatively short and easy, for the passage was sheltered by the mainland coast and the bulk of Sewil itself. But Perian had not reckoned with sea-sickness and the misery of vomiting uncontrollably over the side of a madly pitching boat that soon began to seem to him wilder than the wildest unbroken horse he had ever tamed. Ilo was cheerful enough - singing as he worked, and laughing with delight at being back in the job he knew best.

"Why didn't I stick to what I know best?" Perian grumbled, clinging desperately to the side of Islander.

"And what was that. Sir?" asked Ilo shyly.

Perian thought a moment.

"Telling other people what to do," he said at last. Ilo found no answer to this. He concentrated on sailing, and by the time Sewil was large enough to fill more of their vision than the sea did, Perian was feeling well enough to lend a hand. By the time they dropped anchor he was joining Ilo in his songs, as cheerful and excited as a boy on his first adventure.

There was little danger of anyone on Sewil recognising Perian. He had neglected ever to visit the Islands since he had been king and the islanders were less able than the rest of his subjects to journey to Lavrum for special feasts and celebrations. He gazed at the low evening hills of Sewil, the blue smoke curling from the roofs of the houses, and sighed.

"What's wrong, Sir?"

"Oh, nothing you need worry about, Ilo. Just wishing I'd been here before. Let's get this baggage ashore, eh?"

"You do worry a lot, though," the boy persisted.

"Do I?" asked Perian, shouldering the larger of their two bundles and stepping into the waves with his britches rolled up to the knee. "Getting old, I expect. Worrying whether I'll remember what it was I was going to do next!"

Ilo shook his head.

"No. When you worry, or dream, when your eyes go far-off, you look younger. Happier, too."

Perian stared at him as they halted on the shore to put their boots on.

"Dream, do I? Just like Montague!"

"Pardon, Sir?"

They set off towards the cluster of houses, in front of which a small crowd was gathering to meet the travellers.

"Well, Ilo, one of my uncles was all for sitting quietly wherever you happened to be and getting on with whatever jobs happened to come your way. Safe, he was, and solid. His brother…"

"Yes, Sir?"

"His brother wasn't safe, not in that way. I mean, you could trust him all right, with your life. But he'd be off and away, up a mountain to look at a flower or a sunset. Or he'd sing a song and dance for joy in the morning. That was my uncle Montague. I get my dreaming from him, I think."

And there on the quiet beach Perian heard again the crying of the endless mountain wind and felt his heart warm with the blessing of the magic spring. Then he sighed again. "But it doesn't get the weeding done, Ilo, no doubt of that. I begin to think I've left too much undone, looking at flowers and mountains or even at shadows and dreams."

Ilo was spared the need to answer, for soon they were meeting the people of Sewil, among them the Elder of the village who greeted them courteously.

"Greetings, travellers. It is good to welcome guests so late in the year. I trust you have had a good crossing from the mainland."

Perian smiled.

"A little unpleasant for one unaccustomed to sea-travel. But my captain here had a firm hand on the tiller."

The Elder bowed gravely to Ilo.

"How may we serve you?" he asked.

"We should like to stay here with you for a time, before continuing our voyage. Will you allow that?"

"Gladly. We have no inns here, but someone will find room for you."

He looked about him, and called to an old woman on the edge of the crowd,

"Galla, you should have room. Are you willing to house these travellers?"

She stepped forward eagerly.

"With pleasure, Derran, if these good people do not mind hard beds and simple cooking."

Galla led the travellers to a low turf-roofed cottage near-by. Inside it was warm and surprisingly large, with little light seeping through its small windows. Perian and Ilo placed their bundles by their beds and were soon eating a delicious and plentiful mutton stew. When they had finished, Galla started wrapping herself up in an enormous shawl.

"You'll come to the *reyling*?"

"If we would be welcome. What is this *reyling*?"

The old lady laughed.

"Why, it's nothing but a bit of singing and dancing and story-telling, and maybe a little drinking to warm our hearts now that the evenings are getting colder." And she winked.

They went with her to one of the cottages further inland.

From the outside it looked no bigger than any of the others but once they passed through the door it seemed much larger, even though it was crowded with noisy, laughing people. As soon as they appeared Perian and Ilo were the centre of attention and were given the place of honour beside the smoky turf fire.

There was drink in plenty - home-brewed ale and the fierce clear spirit the islanders called *uskera* — brightwater. There was more food, mostly buttered oatcake and countless different versions of herring. There was laughter, and companionship and teasing and music. Everyone sang or told a tale, until Ilo's head was spinning with the adventures of bold knights of long ago or the terror of the monsters to be found far away in the forgotten north or the wicked southland, or the sad beauty of the seal-people who lived on the soft white sands of Sarri and in the wild ocean currents.

"O gentle swimmers in the wild rough waves
What wonders do you find beneath the swell
Upon the hidden sweep of ocean floor?"

This was sung by a small girl with eyes like the winter sea and long bright hair like a flame, and Perian could not hold back the tears at the beauty of her voice and the sorrow of the unfolding tale of the Seal-King who lost his bride to a fisherman and died of loneliness upon a far northern strand. After the silence that followed her singing, he turned to his neighbour and said:

"How I wish that I had come to your island before! Do you have such gatherings as this every night? Is there always such friendship and peace among you?"

"Why, yes, friend. Life is quiet here. Not like your grand cities and palaces over yonder," he nodded toward the mainland, "but it suits us well enough. And I am glad to see you pleased by it."

He smiled, and Perian would have said more, but just then

he was called upon and asked if he had anything to contribute to the entertainment. He told the tale of Prince Athellon and the dragon, which held them still and silent until the end of the story when the cheers of the Lavrum crowd were echoed in that simple cottage. Ilo closed the evening with a comic song, to Perian's surprise and everyone's delight, and both travellers fell quickly asleep in beds like cupboards in the thick cottage wall.

They passed many days with the islanders. Although it was well into autumn the weather was gentle, thanks to the kindly warm sea-currents that swept up the coast of the mainland and bathed the islands in mildness. Life was pleasant here, steadily prosperous, what with the trade in fish and that in wool - raw fleece and skilfully woven or knitted garments.

Perian and Ilo spent part of each day wandering about the island enjoying its wild beauty and talking together. The woman they lodged with was glad of Perian's help with the heavier jobs that needed doing before winter set in, and he carted peat for her to stack in the yard, helped - clumsily - with the repairing and netting-down of the turf roof, brought sheep down from the higher pastures in the middle of the island to the stone-walled fields nearer the settlement.

Meanwhile Ilo joined happily with the young men and boys in their fishing trips. Perian watched him filling out and growing strong and looking happier by the day.

Then one night Perian dreamed. He saw a tern dance before him over foaming waves, and an old grey tower thrust up against a winter sky. He heard the wizard's voice say, "Perian, Perian, how much time is left?" When he awoke he told Ilo they must continue their journey soon.

"I must go further to the east, Ilo."

"Yes, my lord. I understand. Today would be as good as any, would it not?"

So the pair began to gather their belongings together and Perian told Galla that they must go.

"Oh dear," she lamented, "surely not just now, with winter drawing down from the northland. Can you not stay cosy with us here until the spring?"

Many others tried to persuade them; but Perian told them he was obliged to go on, and though they did not understand they were too courteous to urge their claims too far.

By mid-day the travellers were heading out of the bay, waving a last farewell back towards the settlement before rounding the south-easterly point of the long tongue of land that sheltered the houses from the worst excesses of sea and weather.

They were rather buffeted by the winds that funnelled down from the north through the strait between Sewil and Arrab. Far off they could just see the low shape of Sirra, and Perian thought of the seals and the many tales he had heard. They held straight for Arrab, Ilo praising the king's increasing skill as a sailor and Perian rejoicing that he felt less physical distress this time. By mid-afternoon Arrab towered above them, and they could see the movement of people on the stone quay of the village of Portron. They slipped in among the fishing boats, and willing hands caught their ropes and secured them to the quayside.

Portron boasted a small inn, and when the travellers had taken their baggage to their chamber, washed, and eaten, they joined the customers in the common-room and enjoyed an evening of songs and stories much like the *reylings* of Sewil.

Ilo nudged Perian after a while.

"What?"

"That old man over there. He looks really miserable."

"Yes. Perhaps he's not well. Everyone else seems cheerful enough."

Perian turned to his neighbour.

"Is anything amiss with that old man in the corner? Does he need any help?"

The man edged away from Perian.

"You don't want to go looking for trouble, stranger," he muttered. Then he began whispering to the other men near him, and they all looked curiously at Perian. Soon they got up and left, and the inn was empty within a few minutes. Perian and Ilo looked for the old man, but he had gone with the rest, so they went up to bed; the landlord did not trouble to show them the way.

Next morning, in the bleak early light, Perian slipped out, well-wrapped, to walk along the quay and watch the half-hearted waves slapping against the bottom of the wall. As the sky lightened he saw in front of him, at the very end of the long curving wall of the harbour, the bent figure of the old man he had seen the night before. He went slowly on towards him, then stopped, hesitating. The old man was crying. Perian went closer.

"What's the matter, Sir? Can I help?"

"No help." sobbed the old fellow, "unless you can bring her back."

"Her?"

"My little one. My granddaughter, Sir. But no-one can bring her back."

"Where is she?"

"Gone. Gone like the others."

"Gone where?"

"Taken, Sir. Don't you know?"

"I'm a stranger, old man. I do not know. Who has taken them, these children? It is children you mean?"

"Yes. Our little ones. The others didn't tell you, they won't talk about it in case it gets angry and comes back. But it always come back anyway, it always takes more."

"It?"

"The thing in the tower. It takes them. I think it eats them."

The old man began to cry again. Perian put an arm about his shoulders and led him back into the town.

"Where do you live, Sir?"

"My daughter's house. It's up there across the market place."

Perian left the old man with his daughter and hurried back to the inn. He pounced on the sleepy landlord, and pushed him up against the nearest wall.

"Where is the tower and what is the monster that dwells in it?"

"What, Sir? Tower? Monster? Someone's been having a joke. Sir, there's no such things round here."

Perian said softly.

"Tell me."

The landlord looked at him.

"North. The very north of Arrab, it is. An old grey tower and what is in it I cannot tell. Long years ago a rich woman went to live there, to keep her gold safe. And they say some wandering fiend from the desert, away beyond Lavrum, entered into her so that she became a dreadful monster. She comes out at night and takes the children. There's none can stand against her."

"So the old man said."

"Barka? Then he's right. There'll be no-one living on Arrab soon if we cannot free ourselves of this curse."

"You have not tried, man! Why was no news of this sent to Lavrum? I - the king would have sent knights to combat this evil."

"Much the king cares for us! Never showed his face here, has he? And what's a knight or two against this – this horror."

"I will try my hand against it."

The other stared at him, then laughed.

"You! You're an old man - you'd never stand!"

"I am a knight," said Perian quietly, "and must fulfil my oath, while there is life in me. If I die, at least I will have tried."

There was a silence while the innkeeper looked at him again.

"By the Flower of Lavrum! I do believe you mean it."

"I do mean it."

"Then I'm sorry for what I said. You're a brave man. Here - have some breakfast."

By the time Perian had finished breakfast, a large crowd had gathered outside the inn, hoping to see the brave champion who was going to attempt the monster of the tower. Some offered any help they could give.

"Is there any armour to be had?"

"Odd bits and pieces, Sir," said one man. "Shall I gather what I can?"

"Please do. Ilo, will you get all these boys together into a party to repair and polish armour. And will some of you," he turned to the crowd again, "help with food for our journey to the north."

A few of the townspeople hurried away to their homes to fetch the necessary supplies, while the rest pressed forward to come near to Perian.

"Bless you, noble knight."

"May you prevail, and come home safe."

Some of those who had lost children could find no word to say, but took Perian by the hand instead. He thanked them all for their kindness and their trust, then sent them away and went on with his preparations. He and Ilo were early to bed that night, and slept deeply and peacefully.

In the morning before dressing, Perian looked down at himself. His body seemed to him thinner, older, smaller than in the days long ago when he had first learned to fight. His shoulders were rounding with age. He sighed, ran a hand through his hair – thinning – he thought, and pulled on his clothes.

It was half a day's ride to the north of Arrab, so after breakfast Perian armed himself with Ilo's help and mounted the horse lent to him by the island's wealthiest farmer. Someone else led up a donkey for Ilo, with a sack of supplies on its back. He mounted it and fell in beside Perian. A crowd followed them as they left Portron and set out along the east coast of the island, along a track that led north. The followers gradually fell behind; just before he passed out of their sight Perian reined his horse, turned in the saddle, and held Sheean aloft so that it gleamed and flashed in the pale winter sun. The islanders cheered as Perian rode on towards the north.

The land was bleak and bare and grew ever more drab and empty as they rode. The few small crofts passed were deserted and no sheep were in sight. Only the sea-birds turned and dipped over the cold grey water, their mournful calls cutting through the chill morning air.

"They get on my nerves!" Ilo cried suddenly.

Perian looked down and saw the boy's tense face.

"Ilo," he said, "did I ever tell you the tale of my journey into the high mountains?"

"No, Sir."

"Once, many years ago now, a wizard came to the house on the edge of Skalwood where I lived with my mother."

Perian told the story of the flower and the thorn as they rode on. Ilo listened intently, and relaxed a little in his seat. When Perian had finished, he added gently:

"I can see the sea on both sides now, Ilo. It cannot be far to the tower. Let us stop here for a while."

Ilo dismounted quickly, and began to prepare a meal.

Perian sat down on the grass, taking a little food but refusing the wine Ilo found in the bundle. The boy checked and rechecked his master's armour, and polished Sheean once more. At last Perian said, "I must go. Wait for me here, and if I have not returned by dark, ride as fast as the donkey will carry you to warn the people that I have failed."

"Oh Sir! Oh, my lord Perian!"

The old king embraced him.

"Be brave, Ilo. I am a knight, and must protect the weak and the fearful. If I were to turn away from this adventure, I would not be your true friend and lord. Be brave for me."

"Yes, Sir. I'll try."

Perian hugged him once more, mounted, and rode away towards the last northerly headland of Arrab.

Tall as the tower still was, it had evidently once been much taller. Great chunks of stone lay about it, clearly fallen from the crumbled walls. Perian sat on his horse, looking up at the slimy grey facade. He gripped the hilt of Sheean, drew himself up, and cried out in his loudest voice,

"Here is Perian, Knight of the Flower, come from Lavrum to challenge you to single combat unto death; this by reason of your guilt of the crime of murder of the children of this island. How say you? Will you fight? Then come forth!"

After a silent agony of passing time, there issued slowly and horribly from the gaping doorway something that might once have been human. Its size and shape were roughly equal to Perian's, but its countenance was scaled and deformed with knotted growths, its mouth slavered ceaselessly and its breath rasped. The hands were grown huge, and the nails were claws, bloodstained and deadly. Perian trembled, but forced himself to dismount. The horse, shrieking, wheeled and fled. Perian stepped forward and said:

"Do you accept my challenge? And what weapons do you choose?"

The thing howled at him, came forward at a shambling but rapid lope, and reached out its awful hands. Perian took a leap to one side, landed lightly and with good balance, and wheeled to see the monster coming at him again. He dodged nimbly and got in several fierce blows to the creature's head and body. It grappled with him then, so that his head reeled with the stench and clamminess of its body. The great clawed hands slashed at him, and it nearly got its teeth into him several times. Perian whimpered, trying to curl his own body away from his attacker's grip. Then it stumbled, slipped, and loosed its hold briefly so that Perian could twist away and raise Sheean above its head where it knelt before him. As the blade descended bright through the cold damp air, the creature looked up at him, its dull old eyes filled with despair. Perian screamed, closed his own eyes, and brought the sword down to split the deformed skull. Then he turned and ran, stumbling and sobbing, away from the desolate tower and the huddled thing he had killed. Once he looked back, and saw above the body a dark grey mist that shaped itself into the semblance of a woman. Her arm was lifted to point at him, and a faint echo like a distant voice came to him, "You cannot destroy me! We will meet again."

Perian cried out again and fled, running until his legs gave out and he collapsed onto the coarse grass. He was gasping for breath and moaning at the same time. The monster's slime ran down his face and body. The wounds to his face and neck were raw and inflamed. His lacerated hands clawed at the ground and finally he fell into a feverish swoon.

It was nearly dark when he awoke, and turned his head slightly until he could see his right hand, still clutching the hilt of Sheean. But Sheean was no more. A twisted, buckled length of metal protruded a few inches from the guard - nothing more. Sheean was dead.

Perian got himself onto all fours and then to his knees and finally upright. He staggered to the cliff-edge and looked over. The tide was in and high waves creamed roaring against the rocks. He threw Sheean's remains as far out to sea as he could manage.

"Goodbye," he whispered. Then he turned and limped towards the south.

Ilo, left alone, had set up a camp and got a fire ready to light when evening should come. He had caught the run-away horse and tethered it beside the donkey, draping both animals in blankets to keep off the wind. Then he prepared food and drink so that he could have it ready for Perian as soon as he came back.

"If he comes back," he muttered. The donkey looked at him, its head on one side. Then there were several hours of waiting, until Perian stumbled out of the night towards the fire. Ilo stripped him of his armour, laid him in soft blankets, gave him hot spiced wine to drink and bathed his wounds in warm water.

"Oh, my lord, I am so glad to see you! How excited they will all be in Portron. Was the monster very terrible?"

Perian shuddered.

"Ilo, don't ask me. I cannot speak of it yet. But I thank you for your care of me. I think I could sleep now."

Ilo watched beside the king for a while, then settled down by the fire.

In the darkest hour of the night he was woken by screams. Perian, still asleep, cried out,

"No! No! Death, and despair, are these all? No! Where is light? Light!"

Ilo caught one of Perian's hands and murmured to him the nonsense his mother had soothed him with when he was little. Gradually Perian's desperate grip slackened and he slept quietly again. Ilo crawled in beside him and held him in his arms until morning. The nightmares did not return.

About noon the next day Ilo, stumbling along on foot, led Perian's horse up to the inn at Portron. A silent crowd gathered. Willing hands lifted the half-conscious king down and led the animals away. Ilo told the people,

"The monster is dead; my master has set you free. Now bring your healer to him, and save him."

"Quickly, quickly," they cried, and several rushed off to find the healer. Perian was carried to his chamber and put to bed.

"Do not fear," the healer told Ilo. "Your master is weary, exhausted. But he will live. He must sleep now, then eat and rest and grow strong again. His wounds are ugly, but not deep. He will live."

Ilo nodded, and fell across the foot of Perian's bed, asleep at once. The healer left them, and went to tell the people that their champion would live.

After several days, Perian was able to leave the inn for a brief walk. As soon as he appeared, the people gathered to cheer.

"Don't push him!" cried Ilo.

"Leave, off, can't you?" urged the inn-keeper.

But Perian smiled at them and held up his hand for silence.

"I thank you for your greeting. I am almost well again."

More cheers.

"Well done!" some shouted.

"Bless you, my lord!" called others.

"We'll never forget you," they told him.

Then one rough-looking lad asked, "Didn't you see no treasure, then?"

"Shush!" said everyone else at once, and the nearest man clouted the boy sharply across the head.

"Let's have some respect!"

But Perian spoke again:

"What I bring back from that tower is no treasure of gold but a little knowledge. Would any of you share it with me?"

Some looked puzzled, but Barka's daughter said:

"Tell us, my lord."

"First, what was the name of the woman who became that monster?"

No-one could remember, until old Barka said: "Thalia, sir,

138

Thalia was it."

"Then know that Thalia in her greed was possessed by an evil spirit I shall not name here, but who lurks ever in the desert regions seeking a way to work evil against us. It lies in each of us to become enslaved to that evil; and I have seen the depth of loneliness and horror in the eyes that were once Thalia's. Learn to remember her with pity. That will be a greater treasure to you than any gold."

Barka's daughter and some others who had lost children, began to weep, and all the people of the town gathered round to comfort them.

Perian left them, and walked by the sea with Ilo. After another week, with winter deepening around them, they were ready to set sail for Sebrid, the next island to the east.

4 From Here Alone

The channel between Arrab and Sewil was beset by gusting north winds and fierce tides and Perian was feeling almost too seasick to move. He and Ilo struggled to hold Islander on course. Ilo shouted over the noise of the wind,

"If we can get round the headland, my lord, we'll maybe come into quieter water and be able to reach the harbour after all."

Perian nodded, and gritted his teeth. Islander lurched again and Ilo scuttled back to his place, battling desperately with ropes and sail.

Eventually the wind slackened a little and their approach to the coast of Sebrid altered the run of the waves under the hull. But before Ilo could take advantage of this, the sail eluded his efforts, tore loose, and flapped about their heads for a moment before breaking free and disappearing into the distance. The boat swung round violently several times while they struggled to stay aboard. Perian looked up.

"Ilo! The cliffs! We're drifting in!"

Ilo stood up, the boat drove against the rock, and Perian found himself in the sea while all around him wood splintered on stone. He had one glimpse of Ilo tossing in the water, then he himself was hurled against the tumbled boulders at the foot of the cliff. He managed to cling to the slippery surface while the waves lashed over him. Gradually he worked his way further out of the water and onto the strip of higher rocks that huddled close against the cliff. He looked at the foaming water breaking against the shore.

"Ilo! Ilo!"

"Here! Over here!"

Perian swung round and saw the boy clinging to a part of the shattered hull, some way off-shore. The tide was carrying him in.

"Hang on, lad! Hang on!"

Perian scrambled down to the edge of the water and he and Ilo stretched out their arms towards each other, but the sea held them apart until one kindly wave swelled up beneath Ilo and carried him within Perian's reach. The king heaved his friend to safety, and they fell to the ground at the foot of the towering cliff.

Perian gathered Ilo into his arms, and sat trying to recover his breath. Both were shivering, and Perian saw that Ilo's face was blue with cold.

"Ilo, don't go to sleep. It's dangerous."

"I'm cold. Please Sir, I'm cold." And he drooped in Perian's arms. Perian winced in the bitter cutting wind. He pulled his sodden cloak round the boy's shoulders. Then he was aware of snatching himself awake. Ilo was very still. Perian looked up and down the shoreline. He looked out to sea. He looked up at the cliff. There was a diagonal fault across the face of the rock that might have offered a foot-hold to a particularly small and sure-footed mountain goat. There was no other way to go.

"Ilo."

He did not hear.

Perian took off his tunic and began tearing it into strips,

which he tied together to make a rope. With this, he lashed Ilo's limp body onto his own back, to leave his hands free for climbing. It took a long time; Perian's hands were cold and wet and stiff. As he began to edge his way up the perilous path, the rain started. Perian could not hold back his tears. He leaned his head against the rock-face, shouted, "Come on wind! Come on rain! Try to stop me! But you never will!" And he struggled on.

It was almost dark, and the rain had turned to sleet, when a young girl in search of a stray sheep came across a huddled mass of something lying in the wet grass at the top of the cliff. It moaned, and she looked more closely. She saw a tangle of human limbs, and turned and ran into the night. Soon she was hammering at the door of the nearest house, and help was quickly on its way. Before midnight the people of Sebrid had carried Perian and Ilo, bound carefully onto hurdles, to warm beds in a hospitable cottage. Two women volunteered to sit up through the long winter night.

Towards dawn, Perian stirred sluggishly in his nest of thick sheepskins and rough-woven blankets. He made a faint noise, and his attendant leaned over to watch his face. His movements became stronger, his head rolled on the pillow, and as the nurse reached out to comfort him he said distinctly,

"Anna!"

Then he said, "Alauda!"

And then. "Mother!"

He began to wail, and his nurse sent quickly for help. All that day Perian raved and cried and sweated in his fever, while they held him down and kept him warm. But Ilo lay silent and still.

In the evening, Perian fell quiet. Ruill, whose house sheltered the sick, and who had cared for Perian all day, sat down by the fire with her helpers to take food and drink brought by other women of the village.

"The man's strong enough," began Essa, the village mid-wife and chief gossip, "but the lad looks sickly to me."

"Hush, Essa, don't illspeak the boy. There's life in him yet, and a bit more colour in his face. He'll move soon, for sure."

"Humph! You're too soft, young Marn. I've nursed ship-wrecked sailors since before you were born and I say he's past saving."

"Whissht! Peace now!" Ruill broke in. "Leave off and let us and the sick ones rest. It's a close thing for them both; but I for one am glad of this good stew and a warm drink and a seat by the fire. Leave the future until it's upon us; they'll do well enough for now."

And so they fell silent. A few hours later Perian, opening his eyes, saw four women asleep upon low chairs by a dying peat-fire.

"But I was in the sea," he said aloud.

Ruill woke with a start, lit a small lamp and came over to look at him. She smiled.

"That's better."

"Was I ill?"

"Pretty bad. But you look better now."

She fetched him warm milk in a horn beaker.

"Is my friend safe?"

"He is here, in the bed across the room."

"But how is he?"

"Not so well as you. But rest you now, we'll watch him. Rest."

Perian sank back, and soon slept again.

Perian grew stronger each day, but Ilo still lay unconscious.

Ruill and the others reassured him, but Perian was restless.

"I must go on, you see. I must journey further east."

"Now why?" asked Ruill. "In winter? Can you not rest here till spring?"

"My errand is urgent."

"I see that. Who are you? You're no islander, that's for sure."

He looked at her. "My name is Perian."

"That's the king's name."

"The old king. He has abdicated and Queen Magenta now rules in Lavrum City."

She sat down beside him. "Well now. Are you saying that you are the old king?"

"Yes, Ruill."

She nodded.

"Then you are very welcome, I'm sure, Your Majesty. Though we welcome all here, it is our custom. And a king is just a man when he's been in the sea and needs nursing."

"True. And a good nurse I have had. Yet I must leave soon. It is a sort of quest, you see."

"A quest? What do you seek? Where are you bound?"

"I have been travelling eastwards and I suppose I must go on that way. I do not know what I seek, but I will find it in the east."

"The only thing east of here is Mur. And all there is on Mur is the hermit. Perhaps it is him that you need."

"Yes, that must be it. I must have come here to learn from this wise man."

A few days later Ilo opened his eyes, but did not recognise Perian.

"I should never have brought the child into danger!" cried

the king.

"Now, Your Majesty, don't take on," said Essa. "He's banged his head, that's all, and he'll come right again. You leave him to us. Maybe you must just finish your quest or adventure or whatever it is, on your own."

"I cannot do that. Ilo is my travelling companion and my sea captain. I will stay here until he is well."

But that night Perian dreamed again of the tern that flew across the waves. And he heard the voice of the wizard saying:

"You go from here alone. Time is short for you and Ilo has come far enough. You must go alone."

So in a grey cold wind Perian walked down to the shore next morning, a small bundle on his back. At the sea's edge he spotted the bent figure of the old man he was seeking, a solitary fellow who lived in a hut among the marram-dunes and made his living by fishing a little from his sturdy home-built rowing boat and by scavenging along the shore for any useful bits and pieces cast up by the sea. His name was Ral.

"Hello there!" called Perian. His voice was carried off by the wind to mingle with the gulls' cries. Ral did not hear until Perian was almost beside him. Then he straightened up from his searching of the sand, turned slowly, and stared silently at his visitor.

"Good morning," offered Perian.

"Bad. Nothing on the tideline."

"Oh. I'm sorry. I wish you better fortune from the next tide. I was wondering..."

"Ah. So I hear. Answer's no."

"No?"

"No. I won't cross that channel this time of year. Not for no money."

"Oh. Oh. Well, do you know anyone who would?"

"No. Nor no other boat strong enough neither."

"But - but I must go. As soon as may be. I must."

Ral spat into the sand at Perian's feet, wrinkled up his face, sighed, scratched his head and said,

"Well."

"Yes?"

"How much gold you got?"

"Gold? About fifty pieces, I think. Why?"

Ral gestured up the beach to where his boat lay.

"Sell her to you then. Fifty. Take it or leave it."

Perian gasped. "But it's not worth more than five at the most. And what do you want with all that gold out here on Sebrid? You'll never spend it."

The old man shrugged. "That's my business. Do you want the boat, or not?"

"I have no choice."

Ral grinned and held out his hand. He stowed Perian's last bag of gold coins inside his tattered garments.

"Help you get her into the water," he offered.

They dragged the boat down the beach, pausing for breath before the final heave into the water. Perian was breathing hard, while Ral was unaffected.

"Reckon you'll make it?" he asked.

Perian nodded.

"Ah, I was forgetting. Supposed to be the king, aren't you. Kings can do just about anything, they say."

Perian looked at him.

"What do you mean?"

"Come off it. You're no king. You can't fool me like you

fooled that lot of women."

Perian was silent for a moment, then said courteously:

"Ral, have you ever seen the king?"

"Don't be daft."

"Well then," said Perian mildly, "how do you know that I am not he?"

Ral laughed and swept him an elaborate bow. "Oh, pardon me, I'm sure, Your Majesty. I didn't know you. Must be your tattered clothes and your worn-out shoes and the unaccountable absence of your armour and your crown and your sword, Your Majesty."

He stepped closer to Perian. "You're no more the king than I am. You're a worn-out old knight with a lot of fancy talk, and you don't take me in, see?"

"Yes," said Perian, "I do see. Nevertheless, Ral, I am King Perian."

"Time we got a new one, then," said Ral, and wheezed with laughter at his own joke until they had launched the boat and Perian had begun his struggle with the oars. Then he turned away, paused, and turned back to shout:

"And even if you was the king of all the world, it won't do you no good where you're going."

He waved his arm at the wide grey sea. Perian shuddered.

North-east was his course, with open sea to south and east and a strong tide-race down from the north through the channel between Sebrid and Mur. By the time the weak winter sun was dropping low in the west, Perian had not rounded the southmost cape of Mur, but was caught in the clashing tides and currents to the south-west of it. Ruill had told him that he needed to pull round into the sheltered bay that faced south-east, where the hermit had built himself a stone dwelling.

Looking over his shoulder, he saw the cape, apparently as far away as ever. His back ached so that every pull at the oars was agony. His hands were raw, bleeding through the rags he had tied round them. Perian began to weep, and the bitter wind stung his eyes and nearly froze the tears on his face. He thought of the cold mountain-tops and the magic spring. A flash of white over his head distracted him.

"A tern," he muttered, and looked round again. He saw many of the light, elegant birds, swooping above him, rising and dipping, then soaring up to plunge down into the sea beyond his prow, down like stones and up with fish in their sharp bills.

"Why just there, I wonder?"

He pulled nearer, wincing at the effort, and saw white water and a meeting of the currents. Summoning all his strength, he urged the boat past this point and found himself in a current that ran in the right direction.

"Thank you!" he called to the screaming terns as they dropped behind. He got rapidly under the shelter of the cape and then around it, so that before dark he was free of the biting wind and the raging ocean, pulling into the quieter waters of the little bay.

In the gathering darkness, Perian grounded with a jolt on a shingle beach and let out a cry of alarm that disturbed the solitary inhabitant of Mur.

"Ahoy!" cried the hermit. "Who is landing on my island? What brings you here?"

Perian called back: "One who desires to talk with you and learn from you. I apologise for the noise of my arrival. I am nearly asleep, I believe, I have rowed so long and so far."

The hermit drew near and held up a small lantern. "You do not look dangerous. Have you come from Sebrid?"

"Yes. Well, from Lavrum first, then the islands."

"Have trouble out around the point?"

The hermit jerked his head in the direction Perian had come.

"Yes. Until the terns showed me where the tides crossed. Then I soon got through."

"Terns? Late-stayers, then, though they do feed here on their way south. You're sure they were terns?"

"Oh yes, I could not mistake their cry. They appeared suddenly, just when I needed them." Perian laughed, but the hermit said: "Hmmm. That's interesting. Maybe you will be a stimulating guest after all. Come now, you are exhausted. Food and bed now, talk tomorrow. It's the secret of life you want, I suppose?"

"Well, yes," said Perian, and the hermit laughed at his startled look. They drew the boat up above the high-water line, and set out for the hermit's little home. After a simple meal of bread and goat's milk, they fell asleep.

The next morning, after breakfast, they walked along the shore together. Perian told the old man his story.

"Go over all that about the flower again," demanded the hermit.

Perian obliged.

"I felt when I looked at it that I was looking at all the goodness and beauty and truth that there had ever been. I felt that I was strong and wise and that the flower's light would keep me so always. I felt that I had seen, that I knew, some great mystery that would shape and give meaning to my whole life. It was to find that feeling again that I set out on this journey to the east."

"Hmm," said the hermit, tossing a piece of driftwood into the waves, "why not north to the mountain to look for the flower again?"

"The wizard said I could not go back."

"You put a good deal of trust in this wizard, it seems to me."

Perian reflected. "Well, he has never failed me, that is why."

"And what about the dark lady?"

Perian started, almost stumbling as he walked. "What? Why do you speak of her?"

"She has never failed you either. She has come back into the pattern of your days as surely as the wizard. She would have destroyed your land had it not been for the young prince, what did you call him?"

"Athellon. Yes. She has haunted me. But I do not want to think about her, I want to seek the loveliness I remember from the mountain-top."

The hermit opened his mouth, then closed it again without speaking. He looked at Perian, out to sea, and back at Perian again. "Time to tend my goats," he said.

Several days later they were again on the shore together, gathering driftwood for the hermit's fire. Perian said suddenly:

"Have you no word to help me? You have reflected so long on the mysteries of life."

"Perian," laughed the hermit, "I have been here twenty years and I have learned nothing that I did not know before. Perhaps I see a little more clearly now, but it was out there, living my life, that I learned about life." Perian watched the older man's face silently. The hermit sat down on a rock, and went on. "I have travelled far, King Perian, further even than you. I have visited the temples of every god and goddess in every land, talked with the philosophers of every realm, debated with the scholars of every centre of learning. But what I know, Perian, what I saw one day as you saw the light of the flower at the heart of the thornbush, is nothing that any of these could teach me. One day in a far hot land of the south, when famine and pestilence had blighted the earth, I saw a young man and woman clinging together, near to death for want of water. And she had a small child to nurse. A traveller gave them a little water, and the young man gave it all to the woman, pretending that there was more for him. He was dead within hours, but she lived through that night, and next day the rains came, and she was saved. The sorrow and the joy of that sight have never left me. If there is such love in the world, Perian, then goodness and light are stronger than dark and sorrow. I live here alone to contemplate without interruption the beauty of that truth. That is now enough for me."

"But he died," said Perian, softly.

"But she lived. And the child lived. And the rains came."

"But he did not see them."

"No."

"Is there truly more joy than sorrow in this? Are they not mixed equally?"

"There is more joy."

Perian shook his head. He went off alone up into the heart of the island. At dusk he came back to share the hermit's simple meal.

"My answer, Lord King, does not fit your question," said the latter, over ale and cheese.

"No."

"I knew it would not. But you had to learn that for yourself."

"You knew? How could you?"

"No-one but you can find your answer. No-one else."

151

"Oh," cried Perian, "have I travelled to the edge of the world to learn nothing? To find no truth, no joy?"

"Come, now, my lord. This is only Mur, not the end of all things. There's more to the world yet."

"What do you mean?"

"There is another island. I saw it once, or rather I nearly saw it. One day two summers ago, I was exploring eastwards in my little boat. The sun was hot, I was tired, and I had decided to turn back before it got too late. Before I turned the boat I scanned the horizon and glimpsed this island on the edge of sight. East of here, a long way for some, but not, I think, for you. East it must be, Perian, must it?"

"Yes. Yes, it must. Oh, not more rowing. More wandering and seasickness and misery; not more!"

The hermit leaned over and took his hand, kindly, gently.

"Do you wish for your answer?"

He nodded, dumbly.

"Well, then. You will find the strength to go on. Only wait until your hands are healed a little. Then I will set my blessing on you and your boat, and you will go on, Perian, because you must. Rest now, and be at peace. An end will come, I promise you."

Perian curled up in the corner by the fire, and slept like a weary child in its cradle. And his dreams were of Alauda, and of Anna, and his heart was refreshed and soothed before the morning.

Seven peaceful days passed, days of quiet companionship and earnest talk.

"I wish," said the king on the sixth day, "that I were still young and strong as in the days when I climbed the mountain to the flower and the spring - I fear I may die of exhaustion before I reach this far island."

The hermit turned from his work; but before he could answer, Perian grew suddenly pale and swayed in his seat. He fell to his knees, crying out incoherently, so that the hermit rushed to him and seized him by the shoulders.

"Perian! My friend, what is it? Perian, speak to me, it is I, Thurlo."

Perian turned a bleak gaze upon him. "Thurlo - I thank you for the gift of your name. But your friendship cannot still this fear."

"Fear? Of what are you afraid?"

"Of the thought that came to me just now - a thought of death, that death might be the end of all my searching and the only answer to my questioning; no answer at all but the mockery of fate."

"Oh, Perian. Death comes to us all - you should not fear death."

"Not fear it? Thurlo, teach me then - I do not understand."

The hermit shook his head. "I cannot teach - this, you must learn, in your own way."

5 The Pool of Ending

On a bleak cold day Perian set out for the island on which, so Thurlo believed, no human being had yet trodden. Although the sea was calm and the wind light, the air was bitter and Perian was wrapped in layers of clothing so thick he could hardly move. He had only a short day of poor light in which to complete his journey.

"Goodbye, Thurlo. If I do not return - thank you for your kindness to me and your patient teaching."

"Perian. Do not speak of teaching, we are friends who have shared, and that is good. I wish you well. May you come safe to your journey's end at last. I call upon every good power in the world to protect you."

The two embraced, and Perian climbed into his little boat. Thurlo shoved him out into the cold surf, and stood waving on the shore until they could no longer see one another.

Before the coast of Mur was out of sight Perian's hands were beginning to rub raw again, in spite of the heavy gauntlets Thurlo had fashioned for him out of an old leather jerkin. And his shoulders ached and his breath was laboured and he felt every year of his age weighing heavy on his back. He rowed on until noon, and under the pale silvery sun shipped the oars and rested, letting the tide take him while he ate and drank of the supplies Thurlo had packed. There was spiced wine, poured hot into its earthenware jug, which had then been plugged and laid in a lined basket, so that some warmth remained in it. This simple pleasure cheered Perian greatly, and he bent to his oars again more readily. Mur was well out of his sight now, and he had to rely on the sun as a guide to his direction. When dark came down, he would have to pray for a clear sky and hope he remembered all Ilo had taught him of star-craft. He had to pause now and again out of sheer weariness. No terns came to his aid this time, although he did see one magnificent bird, a great albatross that glided low over the waves across his stern, so that he cried aloud in wonder at its beauty. He envied it its rapid progress across the sea that dragged against his heavy oars.

The day faded into dusk and dusk into dark until Perian was labouring under a sharp black sky. Still there was no sign of any island or of an end to the journey. Yet an end came. Near collapse, breathing in harsh short rasping breaths and pulling weakly at oars that often failed to cleave the water, so dazed that the stars blurred in his sight, he heard at last the changed note of the sea beyond his bows. The sound of breaking waves on a sandy shore. The last shore of the world. Perian committed himself to the waves, and they tossed his old boat ashore with gentle care. After wearily dragging the boat up onto the beach, he cast himself onto the sand beside it and was instantly asleep.

Caressing warmth. Perian opened his eyes and blinked up at the bright yellow sun. He pushed himself upright, then snatched his hands away from the sand to look at the palms. They were whole. No blood, no raw flesh. Whole and strong. Stretching carefully, he found that no part of his body was aching. He stood up and looked around, hearing the songs of many birds sounding from the dense growth of trees at the centre of the island. He shook his head; the sights and the sounds and the warmth of the sun remained.

"Well," he said aloud, "I might as well enjoy it." He pulled off his salt-stiffened clothing and walked naked down to the sea. Here he found that the water was bitter cold, although the sand was warm to his bare feet. He looked out towards the west, and saw far off a place where the blue went out of the sky, and the grey winter still reigned.

Coming up the beach he paused by the battered old boat and laying his hand upon it said: "I name you Voyager."

Then turning and looking up to the blue sky, he cried:

"And I name this land Eluth, the last island. I claim no rule here - only let me pass in peace."

No voice answered him; only the birds sang a little louder, so he took this as a welcome and set off along a fair wide path among the trees.

The scents of that wood were deep and rich, and Perian remembered when he had walked in Skalwood and listened to the rustlings of squirrels in the thickets. Here, too, the quick little creatures could be seen, but not running away; rather they sat up on the branches of the stately trees to watch him pass. The birds too were unafraid; they perched in full view in the green-decked boughs and sang heartily. Perian walked slowly until he came out of the trees, and found himself in a place unlike any he had seen before.

It was a clearing in the wood, almost perfectly round, and the grass was short and smooth. Four paths, including the one he had followed, led into the clearing and met at its centre.

Here there was a small circular pool of water sparkling in the sunlight. Perian went to it, knelt beside it, and looked in. The pool was not deep, and the water so clear that he could see to the sandy bottom. His reflection was laid across the still surface as if painted there. He saw himself plainly, his unruly silver hair, the green light in his eyes. An old man with a thin, weather-beaten face.

"Perian!"

He looked up, startled, and saw a figure coming along the opposite path. It was a man approaching, a tall man dressed in long robes of white and saffron, his hair flowing about his shoulders. Perian recognised him by his walk, slow and deliberate, yet graceful. He came to Perian beside the pool.

"Well, Perian?"

"Well, wizard? I do not know if things are well or ill with me. For I have known pain and grief and have laboured long to reach this land; but it has not shown me yet what I would see."

"Call me now by my name, old friend. My name is Crellan."

"Crellan." Perian inclined his head in acknowledgement.

"Will you help me? Where is the light I seek?"

Pity showed on the wizard's face and he spoke quietly.

"Perian, the flower is dead. And you know that the tree is dying. Little is left of what you have done."

Perian fell at the wizard's feet, clutching at his hands.

"But I thought the flower would survive. I thought it would give light for ever, that I would at least leave that blessing in the world."

"No. The flower was yours. Its light was the light of your life. As you were mortal so was the flower bound to die."

"What must I do now?"

157

"There is nothing left for you to do. The time for deeds is past. This is the last island."

"Why, then, have I travelled here?"

"That is not for me to say. I must leave you now. Drink from the pool and find rest. Good-bye, old friend."

The wizard turned and walked out of the glade. Perian hesitated, then ran after him.

"Wait! Don't leave me alone."

But Crellan had gone and the island was silent and empty. The old king returned to the pool and stared once more into its depths. He knelt down and, cupping his hands, drank of the cold clear water. Then he lay down on the grass and closed his eyes. All was quiet.

A breeze started to rustle the leaves of the trees. The surface of the pool rippled slightly and soft air moved over Perian's body, refreshing and healing. Slowly his scars disappeared, his skin became soft and clear, and his hair darkened, so that he was like a young man again. The wind died, the whisper of leaves ceased, and a different sound came from the edge of the clearing.

Perian opened his eyes and stood up. He saw four figures walking towards him over the grass. They were women dressed in long white robes and heavily veiled. He watched as they came to the edge of the pool and stopped. Perian looked at each of the figures, but could not see their faces through the veils. He addressed them quietly, fearfully.

"Who are you? What do you want of me?"

One of the women stepped forward and lifted her veil.

"I am Elyn, your mother, and I am here to tell you of your life. You were a good boy, lively and helpful: all that a mother could want. You left home and found your own way in the world and became a king. That is as it should be. But you forgot. You forgot the flower and the tree, and you forgot me."

Perian fell to his knees before Elyn.

"Forgive me, mother."

"I cannot forgive you. You must find your own forgiveness. You are alone now."

Elyn kissed his cheek and left the glade by the path that led to the north.

The second figure stepped forward. Perian stood up and tried to see her face through the veil.

"Who are you? What do you want of me?"

She lifted her veil.

"I am Alauda, your queen. I am here to tell you of your life. You were a good hero. You found me in the darkness and together we gained freedom, strength and joy. But you despaired. Once I was lost to you, you lived only in memory and retreated from the world. You were a bad king."

"Forgive me, Alauda."

"I cannot forgive you. You must find your own forgiveness. You are alone now."

Alauda kissed him on the lips and left the glade by the path that led to the south.

The third figure stepped forward and lifted her veil. Perian saw her face and knew her at once.

"Kemara!"

"Yes, I am Kemara, the Destroyer, and I am here to tell you of your life; of your weakness, your foolishness. That you should think yourself fit to be a king! A little boy who grew to be a weak man. Who lost his wife, his kingdom, his armour, his horse and finally his sword. You have been a fool all your life, and your sorrows are your just reward, Perian."

After a moment's silence Perian stood tall and looked Kemara in the eye.

"Lady, I will ask no forgiveness of you, for all you have said of my life is wrong and cruel and twisted with your own hatred of all who live. I know that I have striven always to do the best that I could. I have failed in many things; I have wronged and hurt those I loved. But I have tried; I have worked and loved and lived to the uttermost, and you are wrong! Wrong! I will not listen to you."

Kemara looked straight into Perian's eyes and after a moment she smiled. She took his hand and kissed it, then turned and walked away along the path that led to the east.

Now the last figure stepped forward and lifted her veil. Perian saw a face of serene beauty, of power and wisdom. He fell to his knees and bowed his head.

"The lady of the magic spring," he whispered.

"Yes, Perian. I am Siannor, who shaped the realm of Lavrum, whose tears formed the River Siannen. It was I who made the trees and the hills long ages before you were born. I am the Sustainer, and Kemara is my sister. When last we met you drank from my spring: that was a beginning, and now you have reached the end. You have lived your life and now you have come to the last island. Tell me, how have you fared? Stand up now, and speak."

Standing naked before the Lady Siannor, Perian looked directly into her eyes, and he was not afraid.

"All through my journey here I have been remembering my life, my very selfish life. Always I have done what I wanted, without thinking of what others might need. I wanted to see the flower on the mountain, I wanted to travel, I wanted to rescue Alauda, and I wanted happiness for myself. And I won all these battles and gained the rewards. But in winning each new prize I lost something, and in the end I lost Alauda, my one love. Now I stand here, at the end of my last journey, without my crown, without my horse, without my armour, without my sword. Naked. But I think that Ilo and Anna, and the people of Arrab may remember me kindly. And my lovely Magenta. That is how I have fared. It has been a long journey, and a good one."

Siannor smiled and stretched out her arms towards Perian and he became covered in a flowing garment, the colour of a flame; yellow and orange and blue, that flickered faintly. She embraced him and kissed his forehead, then she took his hand and led him from the glade.

Lightning Source UK Ltd.
Milton Keynes UK
UKOW01f1332061115

262138UK00008B/121/P